LOST LAMBS
and
BLACK SHEEP

PARALLEL LIVES

Bobbye Sikes Wicke

Earlier versions of *Growth Rings* and *Bernie* first appeared in *State Lines*; *The Odd Couple* and *Transitions* (as *The Last Rite)* first appeared in *Equus;* and *Take Only Memories* first appeared in *Practical Horseman.*

Some of the characters, locales and events in these stories are fictitious and some are factual. In some of the true stories, names have been changed to protect the guilty as well as the innocent.

ISBN 0-9677652-0-X

CONTENTS

GROWTH RINGS

Hurricane season returns to southern coasts like the family black sheep, bringing memories and adventure, gifts and trouble; some years only a tease, other years a milestone. My first hurricane is a tangled memory of cats and a baby and wind and water, a memory to be unraveled years later and fall into place like a darker growth ring in a tree.

All that was left of the cats after the hurricane ended and my mother's allergy to cats began was a snapshot of a very small girl wearing a sun bonnet and a smile, with three cats spilling over her arms. The snapshot has turned dirty brown, but you can see that the sleepy tangle of dangling legs and tails and heads are a black and white spotted cat, a pale cat that could be yellow, and a mottled cat that might be a calico. The baby came a few months later, but he is part of the hurricane memory, too, because I thought that he would be like the cats, cuddly and purring, and that I could dress him in doll clothes like the cats. He was none of those things. Instead of purring, he burped and cried, smelled bad sometimes, and I wasn't allowed to touch him.

The hurricane ended a lot of nice things on our bayou, where the water was shallow and warm, and so clear that you could see oysters, crabs and tiny worms on the soft silty bottom. Most of the homes on our street had long narrow docks running like railroad tracks out to where the water was deep enough to dock a boat, with little shelters at the end for sitting with cool drinks on hot evenings. We didn't have a dock, but there were plenty to choose from, and I played on the docks

1

and paddled around in the bayou whenever I could slip away from the maid.

Sometimes an old lady whose home commanded a view of most of the waterfront phoned my house to complain that my discarded dress, shoes and panties were trespassing on somebody's dock and I was in the water again. More often than not, the maid didn't answer or the party line was busy, and then the old lady called the sheriff, who always called my mother at the school where she taught before he went to see if I had drowned. That sequence of events caused bad feelings between my mother and the old lady and the sheriff and the maid, and especially my father when he came home. The domino effect of those feelings ended with me, as the only socially acceptable outlet for everyone's anger and frustration, being shut in the closet until bedtime. The tiny, dark hall closet was the stuff of which lifelong nightmares are made, but the lure of the bayou was stronger than my fear of the dark.

Our bayou was twenty miles from open waters, so no one paid much attention to news of a hurricane dithering around in the Gulf on its way to Mississippi, several hours away. I overslept the next morning, and found no maid and no breakfast waiting in the kitchen. My mother and father were still home, frowning at the radio over their coffee cups.

The radio played long enough to warn that during the night the storm had gathered speed and taken an unexpected turn towards our bayou. My parents worked silently fastening things down and shuttering windows. Shingles flew off the roof as fast as my father could nail them back on, water trickled through the ceiling into pots and pans and blew in under the door and around the windows, soaking the towels and newspapers my mother wedged in the cracks, while the day turned cold and dark and as wet as the bayou.

Grown-ups came with armfuls of food and drink, laughing

at the great blast of wind and water when the door was opened and the struggle to close it again. When darkness fell, the women played bridge and the men played poker by the light of kerosene lamps while the hurricane made landfall on our part of the coast. There were no other children for company, and eventually I slept despite the rattling of the house and the howling of the wind.

When I awoke the sun was shining, the electricity was back on, and sleeping grown-ups lay everywhere. I went outside in my pajamas to find my cats. The black and white cat and the yellow cat were huddled damply together in the garage, and I brought them into the kitchen and poured a bowl of milk for them. I found my favorite, the calico cat, lying cold and wet under a bush, and I brought her into the kitchen, too, wrapped her in a doll's pink blanket, and put her in a warm place.

I went back out to see what everyone was walking around looking at. Bits and pieces that had been docks and parts of houses were scattered up and down the street and floating in the bayou. Although the docks and boats were gone and the bayou had turned ugly, all the people on the street were smiling and talking to each other. Those who usually were the meanest were laughing and hugging each other; one of them even hugged the old lady, who had come down off her porch for the first time ever. Up close, the old lady was small and round, and not at all cross.

Then screams stopped the laughter and talk, and sent people running towards my house. The old lady ran, too, jiggling up and down like a puppet. I ran after them, but they were much faster and some of them were coming back down the sidewalk before I got there, and laughing again, although the screams continued. I wriggled through legs and around skirts into the kitchen, where the warm smell of something good roasting in the oven reminded me that I hadn't had any breakfast. My mother was leaning against the refrigerator with her eyes tightly closed and her mouth wide open, screaming. I could see way down her throat.

My father's face was dark and red; he was holding my mother's shoulders and shaking her.

"Shut up!" he kept saying. "Go to your room. I'll take care of it." She didn't stop for a long time, not until he shook her so hard that her head bounced off the refrigerator. She opened her eyes then and saw the people, some of whom turned away, embarrassed, but still laughing. When she saw me, she began to scream again.

"I'll take care of her too!" my father shouted, and he pushed my mother out of the kitchen towards their bedroom.

One of the neighbors stepped forward, then, and opened the oven door. I could see that I had made a dumb mistake, like the maid did sometimes when she warmed up cold things. The oven must have been too hot for the calico cat.

FERAL CAT

I knew what I ought to do. What I couldn't figure out was why I couldn't do it, and why he chose to come here now, to lie on my porch in the corner that stays sunny all day. When I saw him under the back steps, early this morning, I knew it was all over and I went to the phone to try to do the right thing.

"We don't do cats," said the animal control officer. "The only thing we can do is come out and shoot it, if you think it's got rabies." I passed on that offer, remembering a recent incident involving another deputy who, while jogging, pulled his .38 out of his sweats and shot a pet collie in front of an elementary school at recess.

"Thanks, anyway," I told the animal control officer, picturing shiny black and sticky red cat fragments splattered all over, maybe bits of me splattered all over if the target moved. "I'll see if one of the neighbors can help."

First I went outside to see if the feral cat had gone. He had moved into the flower bed by the front porch; when he saw me, he sat up, hissed, and struck out. I could call the walleyed man across the road. He talked a lot about shooting stray animals and he hated cats--once he'd offered to shoot this one. The man across the road would enjoy killing the cat, and then he would talk about that and about other things he had killed, and smile, while I wondered which eye to look into and how to get rid of him quickly. The feral cat deserved better than the walleyed man across the road.

The neighbor on the east might do the job with the decency and seriousness such matters deserve. He'd probably even dig the hole for me, so I ought to do that before I called him. He was the one who told me about the cat, when I half-but-not-really-jokingly said that his big black tomcat ate everything I put out for my cats and dog; it would probably eat one of my horses next.

"Not my cat," he said, and spat tobacco juice on the ground at my feet so he could tell the story of the feral cat, which had been around for years. His wife fed their cats and dogs indoors so the feral cat wouldn't beat them up and take their food. A gentle, reasonable man, that neighbor. Retired military like most of the neighbors, but different; he didn't talk about himself or put other people down all the time. Not macho, I suppose. He was a good sport, too: one afternoon when his wife was away on Baptist business, I played tennis with him and won. He drove me home and walked me to the door.

"Would you like to go to bed?" he asked.

"No, thanks," I said, only a tiny little bit sorry that he chewed tobacco and had a good wife, "I think it would screw up a nice relationship. " I have to appreciate a man whose self-image isn't dented by getting his socks, but not his pants, beat off at tennis.

I wouldn't ask him to destroy the feral cat; it was wrong to ask a friend to do an unpleasant job that I could do perfectly well. Perhaps, when I went out to clean the stalls, the cat would run off into somebody else's woods and die there. Perhaps the walleyed neighbor or the neighbor on the east would stop by to chat when they saw me working outside. Either would say "new cat, huh?"--they didn't miss much--and keep on talking, and I could point out that it was only the feral cat come here to die. Then I could go inside while they took care of it.

When the postman's brakes squealed at ten o'clock, I went down the lane to the mailbox. The feral cat had moved out of the flower bed when I returned, and I caught my breath at the sight of it lying again in the sunny corner of the front porch with an air of hostile familiarity.

Perhaps nature would cooperate while I did other work. There were phone calls to make and a trip to the courthouse; the cat would probably be gone when I returned. There was no need to rush. After all, I had planned to get rid of the feral cat for a year. He had doubled my cat and dog food outlay, notched my male cat's ear like a prize pig's, jumped through the screen on the back porch when I surprised him one night, and fathered the giant, solitary, ill-tempered kitten that my adolescent female cat had produced. Lately, he'd become bolder, hanging around the house in the twilight, a darker patch in the shadows punctuated by glowing green eyes.

Driving to town, I contemplated my track record in animal euthanasia. There was the surviving kitten from the last litter of another feral cat, a mother cat that came with a farm I bought. She fed annual litters of fierce, snarling kittens by keeping the place clear of mice and rats. Once, upon hearing her mewing signal that dinner was coming, I went to the window and watched her drag a pheasant half again her size across the barnyard.

When that mother cat hunted too far afield and was killed by a car, I climbed into the hayloft and found one kitten, too weak and sick to inflict more than superficial wounds on its rescuer. Its response to penicillin and force-feeding was to become sicker and smellier and more pathetic, and after a few days I decided to destroy it "humanely." Injecting the kitten with enough equine tranquilizer to kill a small horse produced a horrible twitching, slobbering, convulsion, before it lapsed into a coma. For two days, it lay in a box in the corner of the kitchen, limp, matted, staring, breathing almost imperceptibly, and unresponsive to stimuli or to the call of the Grim Reaper.

"Brain-dead," my children declared; "why don't you stick to treating horses?" When I decided to give it a hard thump with a hammer at the base of the skull and bury it, the kitten suddenly rallied and began to recover. It wobbled erratically around the farm for several days, then left us and took up with a pig farmer down the road. It never did learn to walk in a straight line.

The feral tomcat was no kitten; he was a seasoned, ferocious predator far faster than his human and canine pursuers, and a likely source of expensive, probably deadly, diseases. He might have one of those diseases now, and last week he had defiantly sprayed my porch with acrid tomcat scent. Time to do the right, the sensible thing, while I could get near him.

In the late afternoon, the green flies began to gather on the feral cat, walking cruelly around his eyes and obscenely under his tail. He still lay in the corner of the porch, now with his back to the house, and from a few feet away he appeared to have stopped breathing. Having been warned away earlier, the half-grown German Shepherd behaved as if the cat wasn't there at all, sticking close to my heels while I procrastinated by doing odd chores. Finally, I chose a suitable spot for burial and fought the hard clay for enough space to accommodate a large cat.

I shut the dog in the house, picked up a hammer, then a snow shovel for carrying the body, and walked around the side of the house to the porch corner where the feral cat lay. The cat rose up like Lazarus, hissing, green eyes burning with fury. There was a snowy white patch of fur at his throat--I had always thought he was a totally black cat. I retreated and put the tools away.

On the evening rounds of feeding cats and dog and horses, I set an extra bowl near the feral cat, and he acknowledged the intrusion with a look of pure hatred. Taking the dog with me, I retreated into the house and tried to concentrate on the nonsense on television. After the late news, I made the final circle of the day, out the back door to get hay, to the barn to feed and inspect the horses, and back in the front door. Before looking in the porch corner, I decided that if the cat was dead I would wait until morning to bury it.

The cat was gone. Suddenly light-hearted, I crossed the porch, checked the flower beds for him, and picked up the untouched bowl of food. At the front door, I looked back at the empty space to reassure myself that he was gone, and a black shape caught my eye. The feral cat had wedged himself into the corner of a wicker Victorian loveseat, with his head on a soft pillow.

I lay in bed waiting for sleep, listening to the call of a whippoorwill and wondering why an animal that hated and feared me drew close to me at the end, not for help, but to die...not alone? When the trees begin to bud, the whippoorwills call slow and melancholy notes, a longing, wistful sound. By May, the leaves have shut out the sky and the whippoorwills call faster and faster. Tonight the whippoorwill's call was piercing and urgent, a desperate song that would not end until he got the love he wanted--odd behavior for a bird that stays up all night and lays its eggs on bare ground, not troubling itself to build a nest. Do cats hear the whippoorwills? Did some tenuous memory of love bring the feral cat to my porch?

He must have slipped away with the night. The body was still supple when I slid it off the loveseat onto the shovel. The angry green eyes had clouded over, but the feral cat's lips were drawn back in a triumphant snarl. Or perhaps it was a smile. I put an extra measure of large stones on his grave.

SEX EDUCATION

When I was five, I asked my father where babies came from. He was crossing the yard in long strides to get to his car and go politicking and I was trotting along behind him, but he did stop, squat down beside me, and point:

"They come from down there," he said. "Your mother will tell you about it." Then he was gone again. I don't remember any other serious conversations with him except when I did something wrong, which was often enough to keep me from seeking any extracurricular talks.

He was the second grown-up I asked about babies. Marie was my best source of information about the world beyond books and school. I didn't always understand what she said, but she had a lot to say when we were alone, which was most of the time. Whenever I asked Marie a question, she would laugh and slap her thighs, wipe her hands, plunk herself in a rocking chair, and plunk me on her lap.

"Lord, child, you a sight. I got to set down and rest a minute. My legs is killing me. What you want to know 'bout that for?" And she would rock and talk, with great whoops of laughter whenever I asked another question, for as long as she dared "waste time." I didn't know, then, that I loved Marie, although I knew that I hated Sundays because Marie didn't work on Sundays. On Sunday she went to church, unless she went to jail or the hospital on Saturday night; then there would be no kind black mountain to hide behind on Monday, no jokes and no treats, and there might be the phone call that my mother laughed about at her bridge club:

"Miz Sikes, you got to come git me. I bin stobbed to the

hollow." Sundays I waited, with an uneasy feeling that it wasn't really funny, to find out if my mother would get Marie out of jail or the hospital again.

Marie wouldn't help me with the baby problem, although she was willing to tell me that was the reason my mother had gotten so big and was mad all the time. Actually, my mother had gotten fat and mean, but ladies didn't say those words about each other, or use words like black or nigger. Only colored people could say black or nigger. The semantics were confusing, except when my parents went away and Marie could not, or would not, stay overnight with me, and she took me to her home in "the quarters." At Marie's house everyone used plain words and laughed a lot, and treated me as if I were important.

No whooping and rocking when I asked Marie about the baby. The creases and scars on her broad face, which usually twisted upwards in a cheerful grimace, reversed themselves, and she said darkly,

"You gonna have to ask yo' mamma 'bout that."

"Why won't you tell me?"

"Yo' mamma's on my case enough now as it is. Go on and let me get my work done."

I knew better than to ask my mother any questions she didn't want to hear, which seemed to include more and more questions as I grew older. I wondered if there was a book about babies. I had been reading for two years and Miss Bertha Henry, the spinster who lovingly tended and censored the town library, kept me supplied with children's books. I had two or three books of my own and I had read some of my parents' books, but Miss Henry wouldn't let me take grown-up books home. I could see that if Marie thought the baby problem was serious, Miss Henry might "take a spell" if I approached her. That certainly might have been entertaining, but I reckoned that the minute Miss Henry recovered from her spell she would let my mother know what I was up to.

Just as I despaired of ever learning the truth about the baby problem, and had just about decided to accept the stories told by the older children at school--which didn't make any sense because they kept giggling and I knew it was a serious problem, a new book appeared on the shelves at home. It was a small book called "The Miracle of Birth." The title was its only emotional statement. The first chapter made it clear that reproduction was not to be undertaken lightly, and by the time I figured out that love was involved, years later, it was too late. It was a scholarly, biological sort of book, and I think it must have been written for 12- or 13-year-olds. It used all the right words and explained very well who did what to whom and how it all came out, but there weren't any pictures except for drawings of eggs dividing and fetuses at various stages. I memorized the text and was more or less satisfied except for wishing I knew what all the other parts looked like.

The baby was a big disappointment. Nothing really happened. My mother went away without saying she was going away, but then she wasn't home before that either except for dinner or parties, because she taught school and she had bridge games and teas and meetings the rest of the time. My father came home for dinner since the legislature wasn't in session that month, and went to his newspaper and meetings and parties the rest of the time.

When they brought the baby home, the most remarkable thing about him was that everyone kept saying "What a *good* baby he is," for about fifty years. It was said often to me in an accusing tone, which I eventually figured out meant that I had not been a good baby. Marie said what a good baby he was, too, and that worried me. Only my father seemed to be really happy about the baby: he said "my son" a lot, although it was only a little baby.

By the time Miss Henry, the librarian, paid her respects to the new baby, he was able to sit up. She came on a cold, damp day when I had the croup, so I was allowed to stay in the living room with the fire and the baby and Miss Henry.

My mother put the baby on a rug in front of the fireplace, and arranged Miss Henry in an armchair. Miss Henry's tiny feet barely touched the floor, but the rest of her filled the chair. She took a long time wriggling herself into a comfortable position and looking about the room before she told my mother how well she looked. With a spinster's sensitivity to biological processes, she explained that she had not wanted to intrude until my mother had time to recover from her "ordeal."

My mother gave Miss Henry tea and homemade cookies, and me Koolaid, which is kinder to croup than milk, then they smiled at each other while Miss Henry studied the baby carefully. I could see that Miss Henry was not a baby fancier, and I didn't mind when she politely allowed that he seemed like a good baby. I knew my place in Miss Henry's heart was secure because I read more books than anyone in town.

She had brought a gift for the baby and, to my astonishment, a gift for me, a book. The books that Miss Henry bought for the library out of her own small inheritance were meagerly supplemented with funds raised by "silver teas" and by donations of used books. I did not know about money for libraries then, but I knew that this was a fine, new book for an older child and that Miss Henry would not steal a library book, so she must have bought it just for me. That secured Miss Henry's place in *my* heart forever.

I hugged my new book to my heart and hung on every word that passed between Miss Henry and my mother, waiting for Miss Henry, who knew everything about books, and my mother, who knew everything about everything else, to shed more light on the subject of babies. But they talked only of other ladies and recipes and how unreliable maids had become--"but what can you expect," they said. While my mother talked, Miss Henry daintily popped cookies into her mouth, one by one like the ticking of a metronome until it was her turn to speak. The lull that signals the end of a visit came, and Miss Henry finished her second cup of tea, slipped the last two cookies into her pocket, and wriggled herself free of the chair.

As Miss Henry wrapped her black crocheted shawl about her shoulders to leave, she took one more careful look at the new baby, and exclaimed,

"Why, I declare, Mrs. Sikes, this baby has brown eyes!"

My mother agreed that he did.

"And your eyes are blue." Miss Henry's own little black eyes scrunched up and glittered like the black onyx and gold brooch that guarded the top button of her white blouse.

"Well, yes, rather greenish-blue, I'd say," said my mother, who was quite vain about her large, smoky eyes.

"And I believe Mr. Sikes has blue eyes, too," Miss Henry persisted, and again my mother agreed.

"Well, I declare!" crowed Miss Henry, triumphantly. "Then this baby must take after his father!"

SOUTHERN MEN FROM TWILIGHT TO DARK

Kate had to slam the battered mailbox twice to close it. She ought to replace it--if it ever got to the top of her list of things to fix or replace. An urgent whinny answered the second slam and sent an unpleasant shiver down her back. Slamming the mailbox did not ordinarily evoke equine comment: an ectopic whinny usually meant trouble. She scrambled back into the pick-up, coasted down the hill and into her driveway between the barn and the house.

The horses were stretching their necks over the fence to a man. With relief, she recognized the ramrod slender figure of Jim King, waved, and drove past him to park near the kitchen door. King had left an unwelcome message on her answering machine yesterday, booming over the wires in the way of the slightly deaf and sounding angry when he said that he didn't believe he would take the colt, he would be in touch.

Maybe he had come to say he would buy the colt after all. She took heart at the sight of a red lead rope lying on the trunk of his car; he must have been handling the colt.

She'd be a fool to get her hopes up again; she ought to be angry that he'd kept her waiting six weeks to be paid for the colt and then changed his mind. Next time she'd get a deposit. Leaving her handbag and mail in the truck, she walked down the driveway towards the barn, still dressed for the office in her favorite melon-colored suit and chocolate silk blouse. Not that she was sure that the old man really saw her, any more than he heard half of what she said, but it might be to her advantage not to be in frayed jeans and a faded, shapeless sweatshirt.

15

"I hope you don't mind, Katherine. I was out this way."

"Of course not. And it's Kate, just plain Kate. How are you, Jim?" She took his unresponsive hand and let it go quickly. He looked embarrassed and uncomfortable.

"Fine, fine," Jim King said. "I wanted to talk to you about the colt. I have called everywhere trying to find a place to board him. I even went up to Candor, thirty miles, where a lady has--what is that breed--"

"Morgans," she supplied, and waited for him to go on telling the story he'd told her two weeks ago.

"That's it, Morgans. Well, she told me on the phone that she was always there on the farm, and she wanted $80 a month just to turn him out in a pasture while he grew up some--"

Kate interrupted him: "You can't maintain a growing youngster on grass in this area; he'd become stunted and rickety. That's too much money for turnout board, anyway."

He nodded agreeably. "So I drove up there to see what the place was like, but I didn't call first and I don't know whether that was a good idea or not."

"Probably was."

"There wasn't anybody on the whole place--it's a big farm--I waited there for over an hour and she never did come home." He changed the subject so abruptly that Kate had to ask him to repeat what he'd said.

"The colt, I said I believe the colt has grown since I last saw him."

"I believe he has," she agreed.

"He's just perfect, isn't he? I can't find anything wrong with him." Jim King sounded angry again.

"He is awfully good," she assured him. "I can't fault him."

"Yes, yes. By the way, do you know the magazine Southern Life?"

"Sure."

"I just learned my picture is in the new issue. With the hunt-

-it was a drag hunt, which I quite enjoyed--it's a three-page article. There's a picture of a little six-year-old girl on her pony and me on Soldier, and the caption says 'The oldest and the youngest ride with the hunt.'"

"That's lovely," Kate told him. "I'd like to see it."

"I don't know why they'd want to take a picture of an old duck like me."

"They probably thought you were the best-looking old duck there."

Smiling broadly, Jim King turned back to the fence and watched the colt playing stallion games with another yearling until they galloped away. Then he studied the back pasture...trying to picture what? Kate wondered. He was a fine-looking old gentleman, with his military bearing, gentle, lightly-lined face, clear blue eyes that often looked wistful, and a neat cap of baby-fine white hair curling against the nape of his neck.

"Do the horses keep the pasture like that?" he asked.

"Like what?"

"So neat and clean."

Kate laughed. "No way."

"What do you do, get a farmer to come in and take care of it?"

"No, I take care of it myself, mow it, pull up the crotalaria and nightshade when they come up, do everything. Pasture management's one of the things I do best."

"It's so much work," he sighed.

"Yes, but I enjoy it."

"I always had a farm," he said. "Everywhere I was stationed I lived in the country with land around me, until last year."

"I couldn't live in town," Kate said. "The happiest I've ever been was when I had a 187-acre farm with forests on two sides and a broad creek along the back. I just wallowed in all the space!"

"I ought to have some space!" he cried angrily. He turned away and glared at the back pasture.

Kate could not think of anything to say. After a few moments, he began to talk about a hunt he had belonged to in northern New Jersey, across the Hudson: it was beautiful country forty years ago, all farms separated by stone walls and country lanes, "but now you wouldn't know it was ever there." The sun slipped behind the barn and the chilled breeze made the back of Kate's neck ache. She wanted to go to her kitchen and pour scotch over ice, throw her suit and blouse and bra and stockings on her bedroom floor, and put on her frayed jeans and faded sweatshirt.

First, she had to settle this business about the colt. Waiting six weeks for Jim King to find a place to keep him and pay her had been stupid. When he paused in his narrative about paradise lost, she asked him:

"What do you think about my offer to keep the colt, full board, for $80 a month? That's at cost, I can't do any better than that."

"You don't have any idea how long you will be here?"

"It could be six weeks or six months, there's no way to tell when the people who want to buy my place will sell their house." She looked into King's face. King looked at the colt. She went on persuasively:

"The buyers are willing to keep him--it would be the safest place for him."

"Which horse are you leaving with them?

"The two-year-old filly, and they have an old mare, over 20 years old, very quiet." She tried again to catch his eye but he would not look at her.

"It's not me," he said. "It's my wife--she's against me getting the colt." He turned towards her, quivering with outrage, and cried out in the voice that she had heard on her answering machine:

"They think I'm a crazy old man! An old fool who ought to stay home and play bridge and golf and rot!" He was sputtering in her face, standing so close that she could have put her arms around him and hidden his red, humiliated face against her shoulder.

"I'm sorry," she said. She gave his arm a comforting squeeze, and leaned on the fence, watching the horses. She ought to tell him that a good horse was a hell of a lot harder to find than a good wife. Instead, she said over her shoulder,

"Doesn't your wife know that there are a lot worse things for retired fellows to fool around with than horses?"

Jim King's eyes widened in proper shock, then he began to chuckle, an odd rusty sound, then he laughed until his eyes were streaming. He took an immaculate handkerchief out of his pocket and wiped his eyes, still chortling.

I'm sorry about the colt," he said. She nodded, which was as much grace as she could muster.

"I will keep in touch with you, Katherine," he said, offering her a warm, firm hand and wistful blue eyes.

"Please do."

She retrieved her handbag and mail from the truck and let herself into the kitchen, hearing Jim King's car door close and the car move slowly away, the sound of two months of mortgage payments slipping out of her driveway.

Beer would be more sensible than scotch on an empty stomach. In one practiced move she plunked her handbag and mail on the counter top with her left hand, opened the refrigerator with her right and scooped up a beer. She popped the tab, raised the can to her mouth, and someone pounded on the kitchen door. Someone who knew that her old house swallowed sounds and visitors needed to make a lot of noise, not a stranger who could be quickly dispatched. Didn't people here ever phone before they dropped in? When the men did phone--because it wasn't convenient to just drop in, she supposed--they always said, "Did I wake you up?"--no matter what the time of day or night--a question that had begun to evoke instant fury in her.

She peeked through the window at the black Cadillac that had slipped into her driveway, and opened the door to Larry Cole.

"Hi, what a surprise," she said. "I just got in. Would you like a beer?"

"I dunno. I'm not much of a beer drinker, you know, and I haven't eaten. Maybe half a beer."

Larry sat down at the table by the kitchen bay window--everyone stopped in her kitchen, always had. Kate rarely saw its chronic disorder until after people left, when she sometimes thought perversely that she had a perfectly good living room to sit in, but no room for living. She got a glass out of the dishwasher, poured half her beer into it, and gave it to Larry Cole. He nodded his thanks, taking tiny sips from the glass and frowning at her kitchen.

"Are you ready for me to paint this room for you?"

Kate sighed. She loved her kitchen. Through the east bay window, which overlooked a deck shaded by a giant pecan tree, she could watch the horses at the barn; through the north window over the sink she could see all the pastures and woods. A large laundry and tool room were hidden behind a door on the west, next to another door that opened onto a small covered porch and a perennial flower garden she had wrestled from the bottomless sand. The fireplace on the south side was lined with floor to ceiling bookcases. She did not see the torn linoleum, worn cabinets, dingy walls and the loose panes in the north window over the sink until Larry came by--then she wished the kitchen was freshly painted and floored so others could see why it was beautiful to her. However, paint and time were luxuries for which she was not willing to be indebted to Larry.

"Not just yet," she said easily. "I'd offer you supper, but I have to feed the horses first and it would have to be scrambled eggs tonight."

"No, thanks. I had to pick up some car parts at the junkyard and I thought I'd just swing by and see how you are doing."

"Nothing new here," Kate said."Did you have any traffic today?" Since Larry was an on-site broker for a new townhouse project, they talked mostly about the depressed local real estate market and the occasional old house he renovated. When they first met, she had been drawn to him by those shared interests. He was a pleasant, polished and immaculately dressed man whom women seemed to find attractive, but Kate was put off by his pot belly and protuberant, slightly walleyed, pale blue eyes--she was never sure which eye to look into.

For weeks, Larry had been in the throes of turning 50, dredging up failed loves, fear of impotence, old financial successes, a recent bankruptcy and the long haul to attain a former pinnacle, until Kate knew the stories by heart. Catharsis left him refreshed and revived, but left Kate baffled at her own annoyance and frustration. It was not that she did not understand and sympathize; she, too, had known successes and losses and despaired of recapturing the good life. After Larry went cheerfully on his way, refreshed by unburdening himself, she had to unclench her jaw and remind herself that friends listen to each other's troubles.

"As a matter of fact, I had a very interesting day," he said smugly.

"Really? What happened?"

"Well, first of all I did have some traffic, and second, I spent half the day with a most interesting woman."

"Interesting *and* a buyer?"

"Maybe both. Actually, this is the third time I've seen her.

She came by last Wednesday and went through the new model. She's an Englishwoman, a widow who lives in the Pines Country Club. I was absolutely fascinated by her, and I asked her all the usual things, trying to get a handle on what she was all about. I didn't learn anything about her--she is a master at not divulging anything about herself--but I didn't care, I just wanted her to keep on talking."

"This is serious."

"I have no idea how old she is, maybe 70."

"C'mon Larry, I didn't know you were cut out to be a gigolo."

"Oh, I don't know," he said, not at all amused."The remarkable thing was that while she went away on Wednesday without telling me anything except her last name--Higgins, Mrs. Higgins is all she said, she came back on Thursday. On Thursday she spent another hour going over the townhouse, asked all the right questions, and then she asked what changes the builders were willing to make in an unfinished model."

"That sounds very encouraging."

"And when she went away the second time, I still did not know anything about her. Her phone number isn't listed and she's not in the city directory."

"Why didn't you ask her?"

"I did. She said "Why would you want to know that?" and I felt like a fool trying to explain how we work by following up drop-ins. Then she showed up today, driving a convertible and wearing white overalls and a red hat, for God's sake."

"Why shouldn't an older woman drive a convertible and wear white overalls and a red hat?"

"Well, I don't know. I guess there's no reason. She really looked pretty good. She stayed all morning and I would have taken her to lunch if I hadn't already had an appointment. I bring my guitar to the site so I can practice if nobody comes by, and she saw it and asked me to play for her."

"And?"

"I did. And she asked if W. L. Cole, Jr. was related to me, and I said he was my son, and she said that he had buried her husband and she'd arranged for him to bury her, too."

"What is this, *All in the Family*?"

"Sounds like it, doesn't it? I am still absolutely fascinated by her, and I still don't know anything about her except that my son buried her husband."

"Well, this is a most intriguing story, but I've got to change clothes and feed the horses. Want to come along?" Kate asked, pushing her chair back.

"Sure. I'll give you a hand."

When she returned to the kitchen in almost-dirty-enough-to-wash jeans and sweatshirt, Larry asked,"You going to need help breeding any mares?"

"Not this time of year." His fascination with breeding horses irritated her. The first time he'd come out when she was breeding her stallion to visiting mares, she thought his curiosity was normal; during the following months she decided it was sick--after all, he'd been live-in lover to a very pretty woman until recently. Breeding was only a business that brought in a little extra money and kept her ancient stallion content. Besides, as good as her old stallion was, there were no interesting variations, no music or drinks. Just a quick, affectionate, king-sized screwing.

Larry filled and carried water buckets while she put horses in their stalls and fed them, and when they were finished she walked with him to his car. He put his arms around her and pressed his little round stomach against her tentatively. It was an astonishing change in their arms' length relationship.

"Come over to my place and I'll cook dinner for you," he murmured.

"I'm really tired tonight--how about another time? I didn't

know you could cook."

"I have a lot of hidden talents. How'd you like to have a great big orgasm?"

"That's the best offer I've had all year," she said, as if she were declining a piece of stale cake. "Can I take a raincheck on that, too?"

After Larry drove away, she contemplated stale leftovers that ought to go to the dog, if she had a dog anymore, and thought about Larry's proposition--supposing that he was not, after all, acting out a fantasy triggered by the elusive Mrs. Higgins of the red hat and white overalls. Uncovering the uniformly grey contents of the dishes in the refrigerator made her stomach knot in revulsion; she wished that Larry would send her a hot home-cooked meal immediately and make love to Mrs. Higgins.

A familiar light tap on the door broke through her thoughts-- were people lined up down the road waiting to knock on her door? She snatched the door open without bothering to turn on the porch light, and said:

"You might as well come on in, everyone else has."

The tall man on her porch looked startled--he often looked startled at things she said which were quite ordinary.

"Are you doing something? I was just passing by and I thought I'd stop in and see how you were doing."

"I'm doing fine, Carl. I was joking because I've had nonstop visitors since I got home from work, but you're the first one I'm glad to see." That brought a strobe light smile that transformed his face so quickly that you could never be sure he really had smiled.

"Don't let me keep you from something you have to do."

"I won't. Sit down. Want something to drink? Coffee, beer, milk?"

"I'll take a cup of coffee." He rarely accepted anything, a

24

glass of water or iced tea once or twice in hot weather. She supposed she ought not to offer him beer, but how could she drink in front of him and not offer him any? That would be like saying: 'hey, everybody knows Indians can't handle liquor,' or worse: 'you're not good enough for me to offer you a drink.' Of course, he never said he was an Indian, although he often said that "my people" did things certain ways, and everyone knew all the Chavises in this area were Lumbee Indians.

Two years ago, writing an article about the Lumbees, she had visited the newspaper, college and government offices in the village that had always been Lumbee. Wherever she entered, people became silent and alert, like deer ready to take flight. She talked to hundreds of them. Hardly any talked to her. Most just stared at her from behind a barricade Lumbees could instantly erect in their eyes. Carl Chavis had the same eyes. The Lumbees that would talk told anecdotes and recited poems to her, and did not answer any of her questions. In the end, she sat and studied the Lumbees, with their Asiatic cheekbones and their blond and red and black hair mixed up crazily with their rosy skin and barricaded blue and green and black eyes, while they went about their business as if she were not there. She read the sparse literature available on the dark history of the strange tribe that had intermarried with whites so long ago that they had no language or culture of their own, that would never forgive whites for turning on them 200 years later and treating them like blacks, then put her article together from folklore and conflicting history books.

The first time Carl appeared on her doorstep, she was a little afraid of him. She soon realized that he was also afraid of her for reasons she could not fathom. He was different from the other men she knew: he was lean and hard all over and he moved with an awkward, self-conscious grace. His hair and beard were short, curly, black laced with gray, and his beard was always the same, as if it only grew so far and stopped and never needed trimming. Individually, his features were handsome; collectively, they made up a seamed face that was sometimes ugly, sometimes attractive, with dark, slightly rosy skin and those distinctive cheekbones. His eyes were green, direct and sardonic, although his manner was deferential. He was a serious man, and he worked harder than any man she knew, rarely staying for more than a few minutes whenever he stopped, always unannounced, at her farm. There was a dark intensity in him which she did not care to probe.

After she had known Carl for a few months, he asked her several times to go with him to get hay and she said she hadn't time. At last, he said to her, "You are not afraid to go with me to get hay, are you, Kate?"

She smiled and looked into his not-totally-barricaded eyes and told him, "No, I'm not afraid of you, Carl," which was pretty much the truth.

Most of the Lumbees worked for themselves or each other. Carl baled pine straw and sold it to nurseries; summers he had a fruit and vegetable stand which he stocked with local produce along with early watermelons and peaches that he brought up from Florida and Georgia in the same battered red truck that delivered pine straw. Other Lumbees and blacks worked for him in a clearly defined, but casual, relationship. In between pine straw and produce, he conducted other mysterious businesses; he knew everybody, and everybody owed him favors from past trades.

Carl revealed little about himself, but it came out in terse snippets that he had lived in many places and done many different things. Kate often wondered if he could read and write--over a third of the people in this state couldn't and most were very good at concealing it. He had a pretty, younger-looking wife as reserved as he was, a ten-year-old boy with gorgeous black curls, a cherubic face, and a remarkably outgoing personality, and two quiet teenaged daughters who looked like movie versions of Indian princesses. When he did not use the name of the oldest girl for several months, Kate understood that something bad had happened. They lived in an old trailer, out of sight down a long wooded lane on several acres with a Belgian mare, a one-eyed Half-Arabian mare, a mule, cows, pigs and several odd-eyed Australian Sheep dogs.

Transactions with Carl consisted of bartering and trading with a minimum of talk. If he asked for a discarded metal gate and she gave it to him, refusing payment, he brought a gift of produce a few days later. He filled her hayloft in return for a breeding for his Belgian mare (which he had acquired in a more intricate trade), then he pointed out that the tires on Kate's truck were bald and paid for the mare's board with tires available to him through yet another trade.

She thought she ought not to worry about where these things came from, because trust and not prying into his business were clearly major items with Carl. Although it might be months later, he always did what he said he would do, and he was always concerned not to get more than his share out of a deal. The gift of a photograph of his mare and her stallion eyeing each other lustily over a fence seemed to upset him, and when she did not see him again for several weeks she thought she had wounded his pride in some way.

He had returned eventually on a Saturday morning with Abner, a white man 80 years old going on 100, who would have been shorter than Kate even if he wasn't bent double with arthritis. Carl had brought Abner to mend a stall the Belgian mare had broken, but since Kate had fixed it herself Carl decided they would replace some rotted boards on the front of the barn for her. Abner flirted unabashedly with her, told her he lived alone, cut boards without a sawhorse by holding a circular saw in one hand and the board in the other,

27

and scampered up and down the steep barn roof like a hoary mountain goat.

Kate climbed halfway up the ladder to pass tools and lumber to Carl in the hayloft, their hands touching each time he took the material from her. He usually kept the cuffs of his long-sleeved, plaid cotton shirts buttoned, even in summer, but today he had rolled his sleeves up. She could not stop looking at his hands and arms.

His hands and arms did not match his weathered face; they were young and perfect. There was a large diamond set into a thick gold band on his ring finger, the gold burnished with age and wear, and a simple, expensive looking gold watch on his wrist. She wanted to take his hands and examine them, and tell him, "you have beautiful hands." To put her hands around his upper arms beneath the plaid shirt, slide them down to his smooth, brown, hairless forearms, over the backs of his hands, and slip her fingers inside his. Light-headed from the compulsion that swept over her, she bowed her head against the ladder and closed her eyes.

"It's hot up here, isn't it?" he said, flashing his sardonic look and strobe light smile.

Kate nodded briskly. When the rain began to fall, she ran outside to help Abner finish, and let the cold rain wash her face, plaster her hair and run down her back.

Carl slipped into the chair recently vacated by Larry Cole. On an impish impulse, Kate took down a bright red cup with bold letters stating: "I'M THROUGH WITH LOVE. FORTUNATELY, THERE'S STILL SEX," filled it with coffee and put it in the microwave. It was time to find out whether Carl could read and write.

"I stopped by to look at your new foal the other day," Carl said. "She's nice. Was she born during that bad freeze?"

"Yes. That was a terrible week, wasn't it?"

"Oh, yes! I had two litters of pigs during it--16 in one litter.

28

I lost every one of them, even with the heat lamps on them."

"I'm so sorry. That's really a tough break," she said, wondering how much he was counting on the sale of the pigs. "How's the Belgian doing?"

"She's beginning to look pregnant to me. Would she show this soon?"

"Lemme see." She counted the months in her mind; it seemed longer ago than it really was. "She'd be over five months along. Yes, you could see a difference unless she's got a big hay belly."

"No, I've been giving them all the hay they want, but I've been giving her oats, too. 'Course, the oats have run out now."

Kate contemplated another speech on nutrition during pregnancy, searched for new ways to reach him, and gave it up, saying only,

"You need to give her grain, Carl. From now until the foal is weaned." If there is a foal, she added silently.

Carl nodded. He would do as he had always done. No way Carl would pay a vet for ordinary things like pregnancy, birth and death.

The microwave beeped. "Cream and sugar, right?" She set the red coffee cup before him and watched for a reaction to its message. He regarded the cup impassively, sipped cautiously.

"I passed by several times during Christmas. I would have stopped but you had company."

"Not company, just relatives--my kids and their families. You should have stopped."

"I saw a Pennsylvania tag and a Texas one. There was a girl who looked like you out in the yard one day, holding a cat. Was that your daughter?"

"Tall girl? Taller than me, that is?" He nodded. "That was my daughter from Texas."

"She looked like a kid."

"Then it was my granddaughter from Texas--she's only 14.

Big kid." Carl picked up a book from the ledge of the bay window and thumbed through it, stopping here and there. Kate waited.

"Are you reading this?"

"Yes, I'm doing an article on the low-level radioactive waste site they're trying to put in Richmond County."

"It says here that this silo stores waste left over from building the first atomic bomb," he said. She got to her feet and came around behind him to look over his shoulder at the caption he marked with one perfectly formed brown finger.

"That's right," Kate said, and sat down again to watch him drink from the red cup and read from the book. At last he put the book aside. He held the red cup in both hands, studied its message again, set it on the table between them, and regarded her calmly until she had to look away.

"How was your Christmas?" she asked.

"Becky and the kids went to Florida to her family's for two weeks."

She saw Carl alone in that dark, killing cold with the tiny, blind, freezing piglets that would not suckle and live, and the huge, anxious sows.

"That's terrible!" she cried, and instantly regretted it. "I mean that you were all alone. Why didn't you go with them?"

"I had things to look after here. They always go off for holidays, I'm used to being alone. I couldn't stand all of that for more than one day, anyway. Don't get me wrong," he added quickly, "I've got a great mother-in-law. It's just that..." He searched for the right words.

"I know. I'm the same way. But I wish I'd known you were there alone. You could have had Christmas dinner with us."

"I wouldn't intrude on family."

"It wouldn't be intruding--we're not that kind of family. In fact, we usually have friends who are alone over for dinner."

"I've got to go." He slipped out of his chair without moving it back.

Kate went to the door with him. "Happy New Year, Carl," she said, and impulsively put her arms around him, hugging him and patting his shoulder. He was thinner than she had thought he would be. For an instant, he was very still, then he buried his face in her hair and crushed her against his chest until she could not breathe. Abruptly, he released her and held her away from him. The strobe light smile blazed and lingered, even as he poised to take flight like a deer confronted by an alien species.

"It's going to be a good year," Kate promised him. The warmth of his hands lingered on her long after she had guided him through the door and waved to him when he stopped to look back. Much later, she looked out her kitchen door into a starless black vacuum, before turning the key that locked her in, away from the temptations of Southern men made restless by the relentless night.

POLITICAL EDUCATION

The year I turned ten my father went to heaven, which was located in Washington, D.C. He took us along to our fourth home which was, before World War II, a remarkable number of moves in nine years. "Us" was my mother and little brother, me and Marie. Not that Marie wanted to go to Washington; she started hating it as soon as we squeezed into the car for the trip. Her lower lip quivered for a thousand miles, and all she would say was, "You kin just take them fancy new uniforms and find some yankee nigger to fit in 'em, and put me on the train for home."

After we settled in our fine new home, which not only had a second floor but a dank basement and a ghostly attic, Marie stopped talking about going home, and she wore the blue uniforms for everyday and the black with a white ruffled apron for parties. Some time after that, she changed. After we moved to Washington, Marie didn't take me home with her, or laugh as much as she used to, and a root was severed before I knew anything about roots.

I could not go to school at first because we had not been given any kind of immunizations. After being vaccinated and quarantined for an appropriate time, I found myself in a progressive private day school, where the only notice taken of me was to demote me a grade because I was unacceptably a year younger than my classmates.

The school was confusing to a child from the backward South. There were "open classes" and no roll call--we were on our honor to go to class and do the work. I already knew how to do everything my class was learning, and I puzzled over my classmates' questions:

"What church do you go to?"

I wasn't sure. Our church attendance had been limited to the duration of the political campaign, when we went to a different church each Sunday. Church meant wearing shiny patent leather Mary Janes that pinched and squeaked, being poked and kissed by strangers who talked about me as if I were deaf, and not being able to ride a borrowed pony on Sunday mornings.

"Well, what religion are you?"

I didn't know the answer to that either. I not only didn't *belong* to any of the churches we campaigned, I couldn't tell them apart.

"What nationality is your family, anyway?"

I had to look up 'nationality' in the dictionary. Before Washington, there had been only three kinds of people: white; colored, who were part of the family; and poor white trash, who were an embarrassment.

It was all right to ask those questions in Washington then, and adult neighbors asked me the same questions. Washington was still a small Southern town where it was important to know what people *were* before being seen with them. It was bad manners to ask adults if they were White Anglo-Saxon Protestants, but good social and political insurance to find out from children and maids.

I asked my father what nationality my mother's mother was, because the whole thing about who you were seemed to hinge on ancestors and I was afraid to ask my mother.

"Oh, I think she's probably a Red Indian," he said, with a laugh and a snort.

Later, when my father's assistant came to a tense Sunday dinner and my father had gone to fetch cigars and my mother for coffee, I remembered that I hadn't finished finding out who I was.

"What nationality is my father?" I asked him. He laughed and snorted, just like my father had.

"Black Jew," he replied.

I could not imagine what a Black Jew was, but I had read about Red Indians. Pocahontas could be one of my ancestors! I daydreamed of being a heroic Indian princess, and shared my new heritages with my classmates and teachers and neighbors.

A new revelation came when I missed my school bus stop. When I looked up from my book, the same nickel that paid for the bus ride to school had taken me from the Maryland suburbs to an astonishing new place, downtown Washington.

"This is the end of the line," the driver said. "Where are you going?"

I could see right away that if I spent my return nickel and got off at the school, I would have to call my mother to come get me in the afternoon. If she was home. Or I could take a bus back home and try to explain. Or, perhaps, I could circumvent the consequences of these actions by taking the bus home at the end of the school day.

"To my father's office," I said.

"Where's that?"

"He works at the Capitol."

Armed with transfer ticket and instructions, I got on a streetcar, a clanging, rattling, frightening behemoth that crackled dangerous arcs of lightning from overhead poles at intersections. I forgot my fear of lightning and being run over and crushed, when I saw official Washington. It was enormous and white and brilliant in the morning sunlight, and the Japanese cherry trees that I had read about were blooming. No wonder my father thought it was heaven.

I got off the streetcar at the Capitol Dome and went up the marble steps into the Capitol. An arrow on a wooden sign pointed to the Visitors' Gallery, which sounded like a safe place to think about my predicament, particularly to think about the transportation system that had brought me here and might transfer me to other places on other days before it took me home.

On the Floor below the Visitors' Gallery, men took turns making speeches when permitted to speak by a man who sat high above them at the front of the great chamber. After I finished looking at the great chamber, which took some time, and ate my lunch out on the steps during the long lunch break, I decided that it was not very interesting after all, although I had spotted my father down on the Floor. The more I stared at the back of his bald head, the more I thought that it might not be a good idea to consult him about missing my bus stop for school. When the hands of the clock above the Speaker reached 2:30, I went back to the streetcar stop and asked the driver of the first car for a bus transfer to Silver Spring.

My absence from school was not punished or even mentioned when I returned the next day. And on the following day I sat rigidly in my seat when the bus doors opened at the school stop, although my heart pounded until my chest hurt and I could hardly breathe. The driver's eyes met mine in the rear view mirror, then he closed the doors and drove on. On to the Smithsonian, the monuments, the White House, the National Gallery of Art.

The Smithsonian was my favorite, and I had hardly begun to plumb its depths when the beginning of summer brought the last parents and teachers social of the year. My mother had not attended the previous parent-teacher meetings because of her new social commitments in Washington, but she quickly was brought up to date:

"You don't look Indian."

"We understand that your husband is Jewish."

"We're sorry we haven't seen much of your daughter. Has she been ill?"

I missed Washington that summer. I went to summer camp, never to spend another summer at home, nor a winter except for holidays. I didn't mind; the Blue Ridge mountains were surely heaven--I could tell by the knot in my heart when I looked at them from the back of a camp horse. Hell was the gooey slime and swaying grasses dimly seen at the bottom of the icy lake where we rescued stones pretending to be drowned campers.

In autumn I found myself in a boarding school in the Virginia countryside. I learned to love boarding school as much as summer camp, even though the nuns assured me that I would go to hell because I wasn't Catholic.

Several of my eleven-year-old classmates had decided to become nuns, but after two years of daily 7 a.m. mass (but no communion for heretics like me), daily catechism classes, having my knuckles rapped with rulers by nuns, being outscored at basketball and baseball by nuns with their skirts tied up, and eating fish every Friday, I knew I was not sisterhood material. However, I was ready to become a good Catholic, and Mother Superior wrote to my parents with the good news of my proposed conversion.

Most of my father's constituents were White Anglo-Saxon Protestants, few of whom even knew any Catholics, and the next fall I found myself in an Episcopal boarding school where all the girls had always known each other. Where I sat alone at meals for weeks, smiling at anyone who looked at me and yearning for the shelter of the nuns' school.

Eventually, I was befriended by two girls who had been best friends for a long time. Rachel and Lila were softly-rounded girls with flawless skins, real hairdos done in beauty parlors, even real breasts, and the self-assured airs of young ladies accustomed to being well-dressed and cared for; whereas I was skinny, angular, breastless and doubtful of future development (although my skin blossomed with prophetic zits), and my long hair was straggly and sunstreaked. I marveled at my good fortune in having such admirable girls cultivate me. Finding Rachel and Lila waiting for me in the dining room each day was a small homecoming.

After we had been warm friends for several weeks, we lingered at the table after lunch one day, talking and giggling about nothing at all in the way of girls who like and trust each other. Lila suddenly leaned forward and asked, in that tone of voice that portends a confrontation,

~Do you mind if we ask you a personal question?"

"No, of course not," I assured her, minding very much.

"Are you Jewish?"

I felt again my mother's baffling fury at my childish claims of Indian and Jewish ancestors. "Oh no!" I cried out in horror. "No, I certainly am not!"

Rachel and Lila sat back in their chairs and exchanged looks. They were silent for a long time while I waited in agony over the strange turn our friendship had taken. At last, they exchanged knowing shrugs, and began to gather their books and sweaters.

"We didn't mean to offend you," Rachel said gently, in parting. "You see, we *are* Jewish."

LAID OFF

"Would you consider sharing a joint with me?" He asked with that hopeful deference which made me draw away from him, and yet want to be his friend, as he had always been mine.

"Sure. Why not?" I had tried it a couple of times in the seventies; there was nothing to it.

"Now if you don't want me to do this, just say the word and I will leave it in the car."

"You know I would tell you if it bothered me, Jesse. Go ahead."

I cleared the table while he went out to his car for the paraphernalia. It did bother me. In the seventies, marijuana had been innocent homegrown mischief, no more than sharing homemade wine with good friends at the end of a hard week. We puffed away and sang to the strumming of something that looked like a guitar but wasn't, and we--all of us who were not part of "the establishment"--loved each other. We *lived*. I don't know exactly when it was, or why, that we stopped *living* and began existing. Or exactly when marijuana became part of a criminal scene where people who looked just like us did crack or worse and went to prison or died, but marijuana was still the same old weed, and Jesse and I were alive and free, and maybe still a bit naive.

Ordinarily, I would have had a drink while he was there, but it didn't seem right to put that temptation in front of him tonight. A joint would be a good substitute and, God knows, he must need something to take the edge off. I had watched the news of the lay-off on television and figured he would stop to see me on the long drive back to his home state. My

38

home state, too, once upon a time. I prepared a Southern man's dinner, even dessert, and psyched myself up to hear about the layoff, so that when he called from the edge of town I could say "I hoped you would call, dinner's ready."

He picked at his dinner, saying that he'd had a bad chest cold for a week. He finally went to an emergency walk-in clinic, where they x-rayed his chest and sent him to bed rest in his motel room. His boss caught up with him there to tell him that he didn't have a job anymore.

Jesse set a small plastic container on the table, took out scissors, and began cutting the marijuana into small even strips. After rolling two perfectly symmetrical and identical joints, he said,

"They found a nodule on my lung and they've sent the x-rays to a specialist. I have to go back for a follow-up." He said it like an apology.

"What a rotten break. I'm so sorry. You didn't need that."

"Well, they take lungs out all the time now."

Jesse lit the first joint, and we smoked it in silence while I regretted my earlier petty complaints to him and wondered if he did have the "big C." His face was gray and slack, but then he had a pretty bad week. Three years ago, he had been laid off by a large corporation in his small home town. When he could get them, he worked odd jobs around town for minimum wage, becoming progressively more depressed and bitter. Six months ago, he had landed a good-paying job with a telecommunications firm here, seven hundred miles from his home. He had just about gotten out of debt when the firm laid off twelve hundred employees to pay for a hostile takeover attempt. Now he was going home to fulfill the predictions of the home town folks.

"Did I ever talk to you about my out-of-body experience?" Jesse asked.

"No," I answered, thinking I misheard or this was pretty

strong grass.

"It was in the old Mar-Camp Tavern. I had just made five hundred dollars setting up a mobile home and I meant to drink it all up."

He drew deeply on the joint, coughed for a long time, then handed it to me: "Here, you'll have to take care of this. I guess I'm not well enough to handle it.

"It was in 1978," he said, "and I had gone all the way down to the bottom. You can't imagine how it is to live to drink and drink to live. It's the only thing in your life, nothing else matters. I went straight to the Mar-Camp as soon as I got paid, and they didn't want to serve me. But I told them I'd just call a cab and get a drink somewhere else, so they brought me a double Tequila with a beer chaser. I tossed it down and ordered another. I don't suppose you've ever been in there?"

I shook my head, no.

"It's divided into two bars. One side is dimly lit, with tables and a little dance floor, and the other side, where I was sitting, has a long bar, brighter lights, and the pool table. There is a big old fashioned safe in the corner, about three feet square, the kind that's on rollers. I was just getting all right--I don't know whether you can understand that either--so I must have had four or five doubles.

"One minute I was sitting at the bar, and the next minute I was perched on top of that safe like a monkey. And I looked around and thought, how did I get up here? I could see everyone in the bar, but no one was paying any attention to me perched on top of the safe. There was one fellow sitting at the bar really belting 'em down. He looked like he hadn't washed in months. I looked at him and thought that man is a goner; he's hit the bottom. Then that man turned around and looked me in the face. It was me. My face and my body in my dirty clothes sitting across the room from me and looking at me."

He might have been discussing the weather, with his voice flat and his big knobby hands relaxed on the dining room table before him, except that his eyes said nakedly, urgently, *I need to share this with you.*

"After I found myself perched on that safe looking at myself at the bar, and knew I had gone as far down as I could go, I came off that safe and back into myself, whoooosh, just like that. Then I asked the bartender to call the Sheriff's Department to come get me and take me to the rehabilitation unit. The Sheriff took me home or to jail every night anyway. I think you know that I met my wife at Alcoholics Anonymous, but that was after those rehabilitation people helped me turn around."

"And that was it?" I asked. "You stopped, just like that?"

"Yes, with one exception, six months later. I was working in Texas and I caught a bad cold and couldn't get any rest at night. So I bought a bottle of cough medicine, took one dose, and I was drunk. I threw away the measuring cap and drank the whole bottle; then I went out for a bottle of booze and stayed drunk for three weeks.

"Getting back to what happened to me at the Mar-Camp, if you will allow me to put this on you, I know now that I had a visitation, and that is what saved me. I will always be grateful for that."

Hoping to ward off an evangelical mission, I protested that he deserved a great deal of credit for his own will power.

"Thank you for that," he said, "but I had the best help in the world. Do you know when I had my first drink? I was nine years old. My mamma had remarried and I was the odd man out. I found one of my step-daddy's bottles and took one taste. Then I drank the whole thing and I passed out. That's the way I drank from then on, until I hit the bottom.

"I haven't had a drink for eight years now, but I'm just beginning to get over some of the damage it did to my brain.

41

Do you know that I couldn't read until this year? Oh, I could read the words aloud to you, but they wouldn't go into my mind. I couldn't take in what they meant."

I remembered watching Jesse read and wondering if he was illiterate. He was always straightforward about being an alcoholic, but I had avoided the subject; now I thought that I had been insensitive. Feeling guilty, I offered more coffee and a more comfortable chair. When we were settled in the living room, he asked me if I knew that his father had died at 57.

"No, I didn't. That's pretty young."

"That's why I feel like I have to get everything I can now," he said. "I can't afford to waste any more time. I guess you know that the secret of longevity is choosing your parents wisely?"

I chuckled politely and pointed out that his mother was still alive, then the specter of her alcoholism hung in the air between us.

"You come from long-lived stock," he reminded me, "so you haven't had to think about this yet."

"That just proves that only the good die young," I retorted.

We decided not to smoke the second joint, but he kept talking and talking as if we had, laying out pieces of his life before me.

"Do you remember telling me how fit I looked last summer?"

"Yeah, you looked terrific, Jesse."

"I was jogging twelve miles a day."

"Really? I didn't know you were a jogger."

"I'm not. I had my marijuana plants on a twelve-mile path along the river on your father's property."

I reminded Jesse that two of my father's major obsessions were his real estate and "long-haired junkies:" he loved the first and hated the second with equally fierce passion. We laughed at the picture of sanctimonious, short-haired Jesse

42

tending his pot on the sacred grounds, until he stopped laughing in a paroxysm of coughing.

"I had gotten an electrician's license, you remember, but I still couldn't find any work. Alice could find only two or three nights work a week, and we had run out of places to borrow money to live on. There was nothing left to do. We had nothing left to lose.

"I would sit at home and watch the sky for hours, waiting for that little red and white Sheriff's helicopter to make its pass along the river. Soon as it finished, we'd jump in the car and Alice would drop me off at the river so I could make my rounds, running as hard as I could with my hoe and my little bag of fertilizer. I never felt better in my life than when I was making that run every day."

"I can't believe you got away with it," I said. "The only work the cops do down there is patrol the woods looking for pot."

"That's why I went out every time it rained," Jesse said. "It was the only time I felt safe. But do you know that every time I had to go out on a sunny day, that little red and white helicopter came back up along the river again? I'd just get going good and there he'd be, right over my shoulder." He stopped for a moment to appreciate my chuckles at the image of big, clumsy Jesse sprinting over the rough terrain along the river, hiding from a helicopter.

"I had to keep checking on my plants, helicopter or not; we had to have the money. So I kept running, weaving along my trail and looking over my shoulder. I could hear where he was, but he couldn't see me as along as I stayed under the trees.

"Do you remember the Windell family? Had two boys, lived near you on Cobb Street." I said I thought I remembered them, which was the lie I always told about the home town folks.

"Ted, he was the oldest, was flying that little red and white for the Sheriff's Department as part of his National Guard duty. And I was meeting him for breakfast at the waffle house every Saturday morning."

"Wasn't that rather awkward? I didn't know you were friends."

"We're not." Jesse looked at me sideways, watching my face. "One Wednesday, he sent word for me to meet with him that Saturday."

Looking pleased with my reaction, he clenched his fists on his chest and said, "You know, I had a heart attack when I was 37, but that wasn't anything compared to the pain I got when the message came that he wanted to see me. My little heart just folded up in my chest. It was a lifetime until Saturday.

"Well, I met him at ten o'clock, and I ordered a pecan waffle. He asked how I'd been. He said he'd heard I was looking for a job, and he asked what line of work I was looking for. I told him I'd been in telecommunications for 25 years and I had an electrician's license, too. He said that he and his brother owned an appliance and lighting fixture business in Talla-hassee. 'We specialize in low wattage appliances,' he told me, 'and we might have an opening for you.'"

"That sounds like a proposition to me! And I can't believe you actually ordered a waffle and ate it."

"Actually, I ate two waffles. And for six weeks I had breakfast with Ted every Saturday morning. He never mentioned the job again and we just talked around each other. And for six weeks, I kept making my run because I had to, and he kept making his run. At the end, I harvested my crop during the night, and he only sent for me to have breakfast with him once after that."

"And?"

"I had to know. Of course, I'd already sold the crop and I knew there wasn't anything left for the Sheriff to find. After I ate the last pecan waffle that he paid for with the taxpayers' money, I asked him if he had been following me when I went jogging along the river.

"Ted Windell smiled like he thought I'd never ask. 'We knew you were doing it, Jesse,' he said, 'but we never could find the plants.'"

Jesse got up and stretched, hitched up trousers that had become too large for him.

"I'd better get on the road. Is that clock right?"

"No, it's slow. It's almost 10 o'clock."

I could see Jesse hulking over the steering wheel, staring down that long black hole. Going home to tell Alice there was no good job and no medical insurance. I could not have gone down that road to that wretched village dying to hear of new failures.

"Look," I said urgently, grasping his arm to keep him from leaving, "stay over and get an early start in the morning. I've got plenty of room. You're not well enough to drive all night. Please."

He thought about it for a few minutes. "Thank you, but I am feeling better thanks to that wonderful meal and your company. I believe I could stay awake for couple of hundred miles down the road, and now I am ready to think about what I'm going to have to do. It will soon be warm enough to start planting."

EVERY KID WANTS A PONY

Used to be, every kid wanted a pony. Then when television became a staple instead of a treat, every kid wanted another Pokemon, another Beanie Baby, whatever was "in;" every kid *had* to have it or die.

Difference is, every kid can get what's "in" right now. And if it breaks, get another one just like it. When what's "in" is "out," its heavenly reward is a cluttered drawer or the trash bin, far easier than a lingering or unexpected death and the excavation of a humongous hole or watching the knackers winch your dearly beloved up a ramp to be carted off and converted to dog food.

Difference is, what's "in"doesn't need you, too. *It* doesn't love *you*. You won't forever remember its name, the living, warm feel of it, and how it felt and what you shared.

On the other hand, Pokemon won't break your heart.

Until I was twelve years old and gave up on a lot of things, I never wanted anything that wasn't equine: a pony, Black Beauty, a mule or Pegasus would serve equally well. For four decades, I managed to forget that sometimes I had gotten what I wanted. Perhaps I would never have remembered if I hadn't returned to the village where I lived from ages 5 to 10 and visited one of my few childhood memories.

Corrine Cox had lived in the same bungalow for fifty years, a few doors from the house my parents had built. Corrine Cox had taught me piano and dancing for three or four years before we moved to Washington. She was unmistakenly the teacher I remembered, straight and slender, with a smooth, contented face, and with a sharp pang I remembered how much I had loved, then missed her lessons. My mother still came to an annual houseparty at the beach with Corrine and other bridge-playing ladies; my father and Corrine's husband had been partners in a beach development which the national media had cited as a conflict of interest for the He-Coon. Corrine Cox's modest living room seemed unchanged since 1940. What had happened to Ben Cox's share of the fortune they purportedly made on the beach development?

When I told her about coming to the village to work on my father's book, Corrine Cox grew distant; she asked about my mother, then walked me onto the porch.

"That man pulling weeds by the fence lived next door to you," she said, and took me over to speak to the elderly man. He remembered me immediately--the memories of the people in the village were astonishing:

"Oh yes, I know you," he said. "Do you know what you did the day after you moved in next door to me? You crawled under the fence and bit me on the leg while I was working in my garden."

I laughed and apologized, and said I didn't really believe I could have done that. The old man ignored my flustered apology.

"In a couple of years," he said, "you were back over here borrowing my horse. You remember Big Red, don't you? You had to climb up on the fence to get on his back."

Big Red: a tall, strong bundle of sheer terror that drew me like a magnet. He ran away every time I rode him, galloping madly down the highway to a barn where he'd once been kept. The abandoned barn had a center aisle open to the road, stalls down both sides, and a hayloft overhead. Once Big Red decided to bolt, there was no way a child could stop him. I could only hang on, terrified that I would fall off or Big Red would run into a car before reaching the barn, wrapping my arms tightly around his neck and burying my face in his mane so that my neck would not be broken by the low hayloft when Big Red galloped into the barn. After running away, Big Red would let me ride him like any old safe horse for an eight year old - until the next time.

"I told your daddy you didn't have any business on Big Red, but you know how he is. If he makes up his mind to have something, that's it, so I lent him Big Red that year. He always got all the horses he wanted, never did buy any," the old man said nastily.

Suddenly I had to get away from the old woman who taught me to dance and the old man who claimed I had bitten him on the leg. Like a page in a child's book, I saw the pony that I thought was mine the summer after Big Red, the summer before we went to Washington. I had completely forgotten about that pony. Remembering, understanding the memory now, the tears I couldn't cry when I was ten years old began to spill down my cheeks.

We went home from Washington during the first summer recess after my father was elected to Congress. World War II was months away, travel still cheap and easy, and there were political fences to mend. Whenever I asked about my pony, my father said it was being looked after out in the country. I had missed the pony very much--it was also my only credential in Washington's fifth grade social climate--and I pestered my father until he agreed, with considerable irritation, to take me to see it as soon as he had time.

I was sure that once my father took me to see the pony, he would give in and let me keep it at home to ride. I thought about the pony every day, sleek and shiny and fat with the summer grass, a white pony with brown spots, not exactly the

Black Beauty of my dreams, but just as beautiful. One day, after I again reminded my father that he had promised, he took me straightaway to the car and drove out into the country very fast, the way he always drove when he was angry.

The car bounced down a sand road through some scrub oak, to a shack with a small bare sand paddock behind it, fenced with barbed wire. My father surely had taken me to the wrong pony. The pony in the paddock had a thick, dull coat that lay in waves over his ribs, and his hipbones stuck out like wings. He stood with his legs spread apart for balance and his nose almost touching the ground. He seemed unaware of our presence. I talked to him and pulled the sandspurs from his mane, making my fingers bleed. His neck swayed a little as I worked the sandspurs loose. There was no other response from the pony or my father.

I fled from Corrine Cox to grieve for my pony, realizing what I did not know at age ten, that the pony was dying of starvation and parasites because of neglect. In my devastation, I was sure I was coming down with some illness. Days later, rational again, I realized that I remembered very little of my childhood: a few books and a couple of teachers, a friend I'd lost touch with, a few faces that I could put names to, and a few delicious adventures that had reaped outraged disapproval.

After he took me to see the starving pony, my father borrowed a clever, well-trained pony from the county judge. That was a real coup because the judge was a formidable political opponent and the pony belonged to his daughter. Snow White was as kind and reliable as she was beautiful, and she would let me vault over her fat rump onto her back and rear on command like Silver in the Long Ranger movies.

At dawn, I would make butter and sugar sandwiches, a

standard snack and sometimes my lunch (but no butter if my mother made them), pack them into a tin bucket with a bar of soap, and ride Snow White through the sleeping town and five miles down the main highway. Except for rattlesnakes, and sandspurs if I had to get off Snow White, our main obstacle was the narrow, rickety wooden bridge over the river. The bridge was scary without any traffic, and it was so long that at least one car was sure to come clattering and shaking it before we could get across.

At the far end of the bridge a dirt road led to the sugary white sands and overhanging trees of the clear, icy spring called Turkey Hen, where I untied the bucket, took off the saddle, and let Snow White drink and splash. Then I poured buckets of water over the pony, lathered her with the bar of soap, rinsed her, and watched the dirty suds sail downstream towards the river, picturing the grey froth carried to the bay and across into the Gulf, and who knew where after that? Even in summer, Turkey Hen was so cold that no one could stay in it for more than a few minutes, so after bathing the sweat and dust off Snow White and myself, I tied the glistening white pony in the shade to eat the tough wiregrass. I shared my lunch with Snow White and if no one else came to the spring that day, I daydreamed until the shadows fell the other way and grew long.

One afternoon, passing the old courthouse on my way home, I had a vision: Snow White dancing up that long flight of marble stairs. With little encouragement, she went nimbly up the stairs like a big plump mountain goat, through front doors left open to dissipate the summer heat, and we clattered into the courthouse lobby. The bar of soap rattled in the empty tin bucket in rhythm with Snow White's hoofbeats as we clip-clopped proudly down the long corridor towards my father's office, and people came out of all the offices to laugh and exclaim at the sight of a pony marching through the courthouse.

At the door to his office, my father was trying to block the views of his secretary and constituents gathered behind him. His fair skin was blotched with purple and his voice choked on scathing words: his image had been damaged. Snow White was gone and so was I, banished to camp for the rest of the summer, and ultimately, the rest of my life.

Four decades later, I revisited Turkey Hen, half-dreading and half-hoping that it had fallen victim to progress. The spring was untouched, as beautiful as the last time I poured its crystal waters over my best friend. With 20-20 hindsight, I realized that I had aspired to National Velvet, but I was only the kid in the old story, shoveling out tons of manure because she was sure there was a pony in there somewhere. But I still love ponies and puppies and kittens - it's hard to cuddle up to plastic and plush and computer chips, none of which will love you back even a whisker.

THE ODD COUPLE

Avoiding the trailer meant driving an extra ten miles, so I took the short cut whenever we had an errand in the city. I stepped on the gas as we approached the trailer, and agreed with the children's expressions of outrage at the skinny pony chained to a stake in the front yard. I tried not to look, but his forlorn, undernourished figure was already imprinted upon my mind.

Once, driving alone, I stopped at the trailer. There were no signs of life, not even from the pony, as I picked my way around the bikes, toys, beer cans and discarded furniture and knocked on the door. I stood on the metal stoop for several minutes, listening to movement inside the trailer, feeling foolish and vulnerable miles away from friendly eyes. Another tentative rap on the door caused it to be opened a few inches by a huge woman. Big eyes in pale faces peered around her, like mushrooms sprouting from a mother mountain, and odors of burnt grease and unwashed diapers wafted through the crack in the door.

"Hi," I said. "Is that your pony?"

"Yeah. Why?"

"I wondered if you would like to sell it."

"No," she said, "the kids likes it," and she closed the door.

Well, I had tried. I should be relieved that I hadn't bought an obviously diseased and worthless animal, or been bitten by a pit bull. No dog, I realized; we could just come take the pony away...an enticing idea. I resolved to take the long way to town in the future and forget the shaggy little bag of bones chained to a stake in the burning, shadeless sand.

Months later, hurrying to a dental appointment in the city, I took the short cut past the trailer again. When it was too late to turn back, the children remembered and began to look for the pony. There he stood: all four feet braced wide apart, his nose almost touching the sand. His eyes stared from deep sockets at an overturned water bucket, and his ears pricked hopefully forward. Great clumps of the shaggy coat had fallen away, leaving raw red patches of bare skin stretched over a gaunt frame.

Sickened, I took my foot off the gas pedal and the car coasted to a stop. My middle child began to bawl in sympathy with the furious comments of the older children, and I stepped on the gas again and sped on, feeling ashamed and somehow responsible.

"Mom, we have to do something."

"I tried. I called the Humane Society. I called the newspapers and the police. I even stopped there one day and tried to buy the pony."

"They ought to be put in jail!"

"You're right. I just don't know what we can do about it. Please stop crying, Mary. The dentist will think I beat you."

"We ought to just go get it one night," my son suggested.

That brought enthusiastic cheers, and the children began to plan the horse theft of the century. In the dentist's parking lot, I broke into the furor:

"That sounds good. But then I would be put in jail." I said the words a responsible citizen ought to say, but I thought that to do nothing was the real crime.

"No one would know he was at the farm," volunteered my logical child. "You can't see the farm from the road and the gate is locked."

"Stealing is a crime," I said firmly.

We planned it over dinner that night. The two youngest children would go to bed early, to be awakened at midnight and taken along. The full moon would be a perfect setting for the job.

Sounds of the late movie came through the curtained windows of the trailer, and a pickup truck parked in the yard partially shielded the pony from its occupants' sight. He made no sound or movement as I unsnapped his halter from the chain, but he dug his heels firmly into the sand when I urged him forward. Taking his tail in one hand and his halter in the other, I dragged him to the shelter of the brush beside the road, where the children waited. He was so light--it was like taking hold of a ghost.

The mile back to our farm was like ten miles, even when the pony began to walk slowly on his own and we no longer had to push and drag him, because we stood out like beacons in the bright moonlight. The sound of an approaching car threw us into panic--no one else lived on the road--they must have called the sheriff! We pushed the pony into the brush and huddled ankle deep in stagnant ditch water, too frightened to feel the bites of hundreds of hungry mosquitos while we hid our prize from the searching headlights of an ordinary passenger car.

When we let ourselves through the gate into our own safe pasture, we were shaking from the damp chill, excitement and fear. One of the younger children was coughing, the other crying from mosquito bites. The pony's steps quickened as the wind from the bay blew the smell of our horses to him, and they nickered softly to the newcomer, giving us new reason to fear we would be heard and discovered. We hustled the pony into the stall freshly bedded for him and waited for the sounds of pursuit. When the night noises of the woods and swamp resumed, we turned on the lights to examine our booty.

In the bright light, the pony stood as if nailed to the ground, staring, with his ears still pricked hopefully forward. He was incredibly thin, greasily filthy, and unresponsive to offers of food and water. We were baffled by his lack of response until we saw that he turned his head towards the voice of the speaker. Janie, my oldest, waved her fingers at his eyes.

"I don't believe this, Mom," she said. "Six people stealing a blind, starved, half-dead old white pony on a moonlit night." She began to laugh, and we joined her in hysterical relief.

"Maybe it's night blindness?"

"Why won't he eat?"

"What are we going to do with him? We won't be able to let him out!"

"He'll fall in the canal and drown!" Mary began to cry again.

"We're going to think about it in the morning," I said. "Right now, in case he really is blind, I'm going to show him where the walls are and park him in front of the hay and water." I took his halter and tail again to lead him around the stall, touching his nose to each wall and then into the water bucket and the hay before we left him.

In the sober light of morning, the pony stood right where we had left him, with a little pile of hard dry manure pellets behind him and the untouched hay and water at his head. A few wisps of hay floated forlornly on the water. We made a hot bran mash and pushed it into his mouth with our fingers. He opened his mouth just enough to let the feed fall to the ground.

"We're probably going to have to have him put down," I said. I'd better get the idea across before the children became too attached to this pathetic creature.

"Gee, Mom," John said, "first kidnapping and now murder."

"The worst part," retorted my logical child, "is five counts of contributing to the delinquency of a minor!" She poked the manure pellets with her toe. "Look, one system is working. He's not quite dead."

"We ought to at least give him a chance," Janie argued.

"Maybe he's just scared," offered my littlest daughter.

"Tell you what," I said, "we'll have the vet check him over

and see if he's got enough liver and heart left to enjoy life for a little while--if we can save him. Don't get your hopes up, though. His mucous membranes are yellow, and he nearly falls down when we make him move. We could put in a lot of work, get attached to him, and still have to have him put down."

Blood tests indicated that about five percent of the pony's liver was functioning, and the veterinarian found him irreversibly blind, both resulting from prolonged starvation. He would not eat now, simply, because he had forgotten how, and because he had lost the instinct to fight to live. To the vet's amused quip that he thought he'd seen this pony somewhere, I replied, nonchalantly, "Oh, we have all seen this pony everywhere."

The children worked on the old pony for weeks, organizing themselves around a schedule of forced feeding: put feed in his mouth and try to make him swallow, and forced exercise: drag him about the stall in the hope that using his muscles would stimulate his appetite. They picked the snarls and knots out of the filthy mane and tail and found a pink plastic curler buried deep in his mane, perhaps left by another child who once had loved him. We couldn't agree on a name for something more dead than alive and he became "The Old Man." The veterinarian warned that we would likely find him dead in his stall one morning and it became routine to ask the doer of morning chores, "Did The Old Man make it through the night?"

To lessen the risk of infectious disease to the other horses, The Old Man was kept in an end stall where his only neighbor was a handsome, expendable Thoroughbred gelding known as Cappy. Cappy's career at the racetrack had outlasted his knees: at six he was the trainer's darling, always sore-kneed and angry at the world but sure to win in the right class and distance. At eight years old, he was discarded because he absolutely refused to run any more.

Cappy had responded to our attempts to retrain him with alternate disdain and fury. Sometimes he refused to move at all, displaying a great deal more patience than his two-legged mentors. When I walked and trotted him, Cappy would go along pleasantly for a little while, flicking his ears back and forth at me. If I relaxed and let him canter, he would stop on a dime, put his head down and deposit me at his front feet. He spared me his favorite evasion: bolting and running madly in whatever direction he was pointed until he was too winded to take another step. That dangerous habit had earned him the retirement he wanted, at least temporarily. But we weren't in the retirement home business, and a big healthy Thoroughbred gelding consumes his own weight in feed about every ninety days. If we could rehabilitate him, his good looks would ensure a sale and a successful career; if not, he would have to be destroyed.

Cappy was fascinated by his new neighbor and tried all the tricks he knew to get into the stall with him. In the light of Cappy's past benevolence towards man and horse, we assumed that he merely wanted to murder the pony. The Old Man paid no attention to Cappy's nickering and hanging over his stall door, or to anything else for a long time.

After many weeks, something in The Old Man's metabolism, or maybe in his soul, began to smoulder, and he swallowed a little more feed each day. New hair began to grow on the red patches of skin, the coarse, greasy fur fell away, and a silvery grey coat emerged. He began to walk, slowly but willingly, when led. First prudently catching and shutting up Cappy, the children daily walked The Old Man out into the sunshine, and the pony turned his blind face up to the sun as if to soak up its warm strength. Then he began to stroll about his stall, stopping at his door and listening to the barn activities, or stopping at Cappy's wall and provoking the Thoroughbred into giving the wall a warning kick.

On a perfect spring day when The Old Man was taken out for his walk, he danced about and kicked up his little heels in sheer exuberance, as if he were a yearling again. In celebration of the pony's new found enthusiasm for life, we decided to give him a bath--maybe his first ever, we joked. He stood contentedly for a quick sudsing, then we carried buckets of lukewarm water out to the barnyard to rinse him. Cappy stomped and fretted as he watched us over the half door of his stall, shaking his head, circling the stall and returning to the door to shake his head at us again.

As I lifted the first rinse bucket to pour over The Old Man, Cappy became airborne. The horse that had refused to lift his feet to trot over cavaletti popped gracefully over a four-foot stall door, and bore down on us with a vengeance.

I dropped the bucket, the six of us scattered in six directions, and before anyone could cry out, "he'll kill The Old Man," Cappy had cut the pony out of our midst and, nose to withers, was rushing The Old Man across the pasture towards the canal. Stunned, we started after them to rescue the pony, spreading out to corner them.

"Wait, Mom," Janie said. "I don't think he's going to hurt him."

We stood and watched silently as Cappy stopped the pony near the canal and they began to graze side by side, their noses almost touching. We exchanged incredulous looks; Cappy was not going to savage the pony.

Cappy was not going to let us savage the pony with buckets of water, either. We didn't get the soapy pony back until the next morning, when hunger overcame love and Cappy brought The Old Man up to the barn for the morning feed.

Cappy had a job now, a labor of love. He took The Old Man out to pasture each morning, guided him gently away from fences and canals, and defended him fiercely from other curious horses. They grazed together in the sun, and when the weather turned bad they came into the shelter of the barn together, Cappy adjusting his quick pace to the old pony's slow steps. The Old Man grew plump and shiny, although his faltering steps, yellow mucous membranes, and opaque eyes revealed the fragility of his health. We didn't talk about the two of them much beyond an occasional joke about 'the odd couple;' we accepted them with wonder, and unspoken knowledge of the inevitable.

In late winter, The Old Man began to fail. Each day, he ate less, and he required a nap in the sunshine after the short walk out to pasture with Cappy. The Thoroughbred waited patiently while the old pony dozed, and when the days came that The Old Man would not come out of his stall, Cappy would not come out either. We went through token efforts of vitamin shots and feed delicacies and warm blankets, then had the veterinarian out.

"Quite honestly," he said, "His heart's gone, his liver's gone, I don't know what's keeping him on his feet."

I knew what was keeping him on his feet, besides the fact that a dying equine knows that once it's down it's not likely to get up again, and I thought about it for several moments before saying:

"Well, we were expecting this, and he's probably had the best year of his life. It's almost spring, though. We'll give him a couple of weeks of nice weather, if he makes it that far without pain, and you can put him down when you come out to do this year's Coggins tests." I didn't mention Cappy; there was nothing to say.

The Old Man rallied in the spring, greeting each new morning of warm sun and gentle breezes with a bright hopeful demeanor for a month, while Cappy hovered anxiously over him. But the old pony still picked tiredly at his feed, still lost weight, and at the end of the month I called the vet. He and

Janie took The Old Man out to his favorite spot and put him to sleep while Cappy stood by his side.

In midsummer, one of Janie's students came to the farm for a dressage lesson. Marcia was a gutsy rider who had made do with horses whose best performances fell short of average. Leaning on the fence while her horse cooled out in the paddock, she said,

"He's really beautiful, isn't he?"

"Who?" I asked.

"The bright chestnut over there," she replied, indicating Cappy moping near the barn, which was all he had done for weeks.

"Oh, Cappy," said Janie, disparagingly. "Yeah, he's pretty sporty looking."

"Is something wrong with him?" Marcia asked.

"Yes," I answered. "He hasn't done any work for a year, and if we don't get something done with him before winter comes, I'm going to have to send him to that Great Pasture in the Sky."

"That's terrible," Marcia groaned. "I'd kill for a horse like that."

"He was pretty sour when he came off the track last year," Janie said. "In fact, he was pretty dangerous. We can't even think about selling him right now. He needs more time than I have and he's not safe for the little kids and Mom."

"I'd love to work with a horse like that," Marcia said, "but I don't think I'll ever be able to afford one."

While she and Janie talked of other things, I regarded Marcia thoughtfully: a small, sturdy, competent girl, as plain as the horses she rode. She put so much into those discarded horses. She got so much out of them, an astonishing percentage of seconds and thirds and fourths with horses that went unnoticed until the points were added up, and unremembered later. We had watched her struggles with mediocre horses for a long time, and we liked her enormously. I tried to sort out whether I was more concerned with a decent solution for Cappy, or with being the cause of a friend being injured, or with a genuine desire to see what Marcia could do with a classy looking, athletic horse that wasn't afraid of anything except pain.

I watched her watching Cappy for several minutes, then I said,

"Marcia, there are some other reasons we haven't worked with Cappy this year, which don't have anything to do with his problems, and I really would like to see him get a chance. I think he has a lot of ability and heart, and that he's serviceably sound for a good rider--although I wouldn't have said so last year. But Janie's right that he's not safe."

"You remember the last safe horse I had!" She laughed, but the pain in her eyes reminded us of the reliable mare that broke down and had to be destroyed just as she'd begun to win with it; it was the first horse she had owned, not much bigger than a pony, but kind and willing.

"I'll sell you Cappy for what I paid for him," I said, "if you really want him. On time, any way you can afford to pay. But you will have to work with him here first, so I can see that it will work out."

Janie was appalled; Marcia was ecstatic. I was apprehensive, and could hardly bring myself to watch Marcia work with Cappy. Back under saddle after his sabbatical, Cappy never took a wrong step. Marcia took him away a few days later, and in a few months she finished paying for him. In more fashionable circles that hadn't known The Odd Couple, Cappy was a cheap horse.

We didn't see Marcia and Cappy again until spring returned, when they beat the socks off the competition at a major event. Marcia shone on the flashy Thoroughbred. Maybe the ghost of The Old Man rode with them.

Did we give up stealing horses? Is there a moral to this story? Yes: for the sore-kneed and sore at heart, it is more blessed to give love than to receive love.

TAKE ONLY MEMORIES

The briefing goes on forever. Veterinarians and ride officials take turns warning against "overusing" the horse; they are very, very specific about the allowable physical parameters.

There was a time when endurance riding, like three day eventing and other strenuous equine sports, went too far in more than distance, leaving destroyed horses and hopes along the trail. But the world of horses is sensitive and over-reactive and, except in the big money equine sports, the pendulum always swings back. There are tough rules now, which will be enforced on this ride with the self-assurance of experience by ten veterinarians and four times as many pulse and respiration team members.

Endurance and competitive trail rides are descendants of the U.S. Army tests inflicted on Cavalry horses long ago. The oldest horse breed, the Arabian, has dominated modern endurance and competitive trail rides, overcoming its small size with its combination of sound wind, hard bone, and hot blood. The Old Dominion is considered by many to be the toughest 100-mile endurance ride in the country because of the heat and humidity in June in the Blue Ridge Mountains at Front Royal, Virginia. We are here with our Arabian to test these tenets.

The final admonition comes from Veterinarian Sally Ralston:

"Take only memories, leave only hoofprints."

The crowd applauds and cheers, then 45 riders for the 100-mile, 61 riders for the 55-mile endurance ride, and a couple of hundred supportive pit crew members vanish into the twilight.

They are a motley crew, from teenagers to grandparents, from just plain folks to internationally famous persons. On the trail, they are all equal because the rules are impartial, tough, fair, and inflexible. Attire ranges from casual to outrageous-- whatever is comfortable and safe is okay. It's a family sport: many parent-child and husband-wife teams ride, and families act as pit crews for their riders. What this remarkable mix of competitors shares is good horsemanship on tough, fit, horses, good cheer, and a motto: *To finish is to win.*

I am a pit crew member. I have been a veterinarian's recorder and a P & R taker and a cook on a couple of competitive trail rides. This should be a piece of cake: with two other pit crew members, I will assist one little horse and rider.

It is our rider's first 100 mile endurance ride and, more importantly, it is her Arabian gelding's first 100 mile ride, twice as far as he has gone before. He is an unknown quantity. Will he lose heart when fatigue sets in and there is no relief? Will he then become stiff and resentful? Will he break down? His illustriously bred dam was plagued with mysterious unsoundnesses that kept her from competing.

Or will he burn himself out early? Some horses burn out from fatigue, others from nervous tension, exhausted by their own competitive spirit. This Arab gelding raced 26 miles of his last 50 mile ride, tearing the skin from his rider's hands and pushing against his hackamore until his classic concave profile became a convex lump. His sire was a relentless competitor who raced against three-year-olds when he was 11, 12, and 13, and won, but then he wanted to be a racehorse when he was a young pleasure horse and a middle-aged dressage horse. Whose heredity will be the deciding factor today?

4:45 a.m. I slept schizophrenically, tormented by images of lame, dehydrated horses and the excitement of the competition. Our rider, Debbie, slept less because she fed her horse at 3 a.m. The heat and humidity here must have been exaggerated; there is frost on the grass and I'm shivering in my sleeping bag. I join the other pit crew members, already at work, and coffee and the horses milling in the barn area produce instant adrenalin.

Debbie's husband, Al, and Pat, an old friend from Massachusetts, are an experienced pit crew team. Although they are very quiet while they check and double-check everything, their energy level is so high it cuts like a knife. We do last minute odd jobs and hunt for other tasks. Almost starting time, but it is still dark and I can't take pictures; if I set off flashbulbs in the barn area these people will shatter into little pieces, then hang me from the ancient rafters.

My camera isn't good enough to portray 45 horses standing as still as time bombs in the pre-dawn in an old cavalry depot barnyard while someone prays and blesses them. There is a miserly lightening of the eastern sky, so I jog to the road to see if I can catch them in profile as they leave. When the blessing ends, a sprightly Sousa March strikes up and the horses trot out freshly, as if they were going to war.

We drive to a crossroads eight miles out and set up with our buckets of water. Still three-layer cold out; there's not much chance of dehydration this early, but we have to be ready with a drink and a sponging. We wait at the end of a straight stretch of macadam for our horse and rider to appear at a 90 degree turn a quarter of a mile away.

A distressed murmur ripples through the pit crews--a horse has fallen on the wet, slick road at the sharp turn--a grey Arabian, streaming red below his right front knee. Not our grey Arabian. The horse is not badly hurt, but he is out of the ride. Soon another horse falls, the rider jumping free as he lands, but both bounce up and walk on. The second fallen horse and rider had set out with Debbie; they're shaken, but unhurt. As I start down to the curve to warn approaching riders that it's slippery, Debbie and Squirt trot in. They're late, but Squirt is calm and steady, not racing. A drink, a quick word, and they're gone.

Eighteen miles to the next hold at Detrick, past Dry Run Cemetery, a name that inspires bad puns. Pulse, respiration, temperature, and vet check for soundness will be done here in the mandatory 30 minute break.

We jump to attention when the horses that accompanied Debbie and Squirt at the last stop finally come in. "Not seen," they tell us.

I peel down to two layers of clothes, then one, then I accept a beer. It's ten o'clock in the morning and I'm drinking beer? Better get to work, look around.

Mae Schlegel, 74 years young and looking fresh, comes in with the 55-mile riders. Louis Rukeyser of PBS's Wall Street Week is waiting for his wife; it is her first 100 mile ride, too, he says. She comes in on an unruffled chestnut Arabian mare, twenty minutes ahead of Debbie.

We move Squirt quickly into the shade and Pat and Al go to work. Pat monitors pulse with her stethoscope and respiration with her hand; Al listens for directions from Pat as he cools Squirt with great spongefuls of water until his vital signs stabilize, now the neck, now the legs. Debbie is superfluous now, and excited that the first quarter is over:

"We came over Milford Gap," she tells us, but no one is listening except me, "and it's a two mile climb straight up. I tailed him and my heart was thudding and my legs were shaking, but we're okay. He came right down."

"Get the P & R team," Pat says, and in a moment they've checked Squirt and written his pulse and respiration on his time slip. Pat wants to have our veterinary check right now, while vital signs are stable and enough adrenalin is still circulating for the horse to move with impulsion, before he has a chance to become stiff. There's a veterinarian free, and Pat and Al take Squirt over to trot back and forth and have his pulse, respiration and temperature taken again.

Fourteen miles later, there is a 15-minute hold at Camp Roosevelt, where we crowd under the trees fringing the narrow field and watch and wait again. Shade has become a major priority. We will begin to give electrolytes now, as well as water, hay, and from time to time, a small ration of feed.

Two experienced hundred-milers are in trouble. One with a freshly bandaged leg stands quietly in the shade waiting for the van to take him back to base camp; the other is having his pulse and respiration taken between spongings for the twentieth time. It's not coming down to normal. It has, in fact, gone up. I watch the distressed horses surreptitiously, sadly, and I am glad to leave when our team passes handily.

Hickory Lane is the 53.5 mile point, a tad over halfway for the long haulers, a mile and a half to the finish line for the 55-milers. Debbie and Squirt gained time at the last stop, but they will lose time again on this 13-mile run. A tall, white-haired man comes in on a mare which can only be the result of breeding an Arabian to a Belgian--a neat trick in itself--and he has woven mountain laurel into her forelock, giving her the look of a large, reluctant bride. He is Webb Coleman, and the mare is--what else?--Arabel. Dismounting with obvious pain, he tells me that he and Arabel were pulled out at Hickory Lane two years ago. He is riding along with Heather Hoyns, a veterinarian on a 22-year-old Appaloosa. Twenty-two is about 88 in human years, and a remarkable performance in equine years.

Despite her slow pace, Debbie is optimistic because her horse is steady and recovering quickly from stress. When I remove his saddle and thick pad, there are pink patches on his back. No swelling--it looks almost like sunburn--and I sponge it gently with cool water. Squirt is quite fresh at this P & R and vet check, cool and dry at the end of the 15 minute rest, but when Al tightens the girth, he rears in apparent pain. Bewildered, we remove the saddle and fresh saddle pad. The pale pink patches? Debbie says that she clipped his back, not her usual practice. With foreboding, we carefully replace the saddle, and lift Debbie aboard so that mounting won't punish his back more.

Because it is 17 miles to the next hold, we wait for them halfway, at a road crossing where the 100-mile human marathon runners weigh in and enjoy leg massages performed by attractive young women therapists. Cavalry riders pass through, relaxed pros who ride the 100 miles without pit crew or any outside help other than water for the rider. Six cavalry riders compete on this ride; Betty Baird, wearing elastic bandages on both her knees and mounting from the off side, will capture the ODR Cavalry Trophy with a time of 20 hours.

Debbie and Squirt trot up in high spirits, having passed several horses on this leg. We give Squirt a quick sponging and a drink, and offer water to the new horses accompanying them.

There is no shade at Seaman's, a 30-minute hold in a hollow in a valley. This lovely spot, which a gracious owner has permitted the Old Dominion to trample annually, is a descent into hell at 3:30 on a summer afternoon in the Blue Ridge Mountains. Our very eyeballs are burning. Pit crews huddle, silent and sweating, in the slivers of shade cast by pickup trucks and campers. It is even too hot to drink beer.

Debbie and Squirt have lost time again and it takes longer to stabilize him for the P & R team and the veterinarian. Debbie is discouraged and anxious, Squirt a mirror image of her feelings.

"I came down the mountain too fast," she says, "and he's off on the right front, he won't pass this vet check."

I take Debbie off to the pickup truck and coerce her into a

cup of stew in the faint shade of a tiny pecan tree. When Pat and Al come up with Squirt she's still talking about being pulled at this stop--"there's no use having him vetted," she tells them.

"No faith, that's your problem," they reply; "he passed." We try to keep them cool and quiet until the two-minute call comes to ride out. We have decided not to remove Squirt's saddle pad this time. Replacing the saddle with care and leaving the girth slightly loose, we lift Debbie aboard and they leave at a very cautious pace.

Pickett Springs is only ten miles, a 15-minute stop in a forest glen with shade and a waning sun. Setting up shop with our buckets and folding chairs again, we commiserate that it would be an accomplishment to make it this far, 80 miles, on the first 100-miler for horse and rider. We have another beer.

Louis Rukeyser comes in, driving a pickup truck and wearing tennis shoes in the same methodical, whimsical manner in which he moderates Wall Street Week. Wishing him well, I feel a small mean pleasure that, for the moment, our team is ahead of his.

Horses on each side of us are vetted, eliminated, and wait dejectedly for a van ride to base camp. We have another beer, silently.

The kindness of the veterinarians when they must eliminate horses from the competition is touching. The vets have been up and working as long as the rest of us--and the rest of us are getting pretty snarly--yet, whenever they have a moment between vettings, they thoughtfully seek out the riders of disqualified horses to explain and reassure.

Here's our team. Rejuvenated once more. We draw the veterinarian who pulled the last two horses, but he passes Squirt and tells Al that it's a pleasure to see a horse look this good at 80 miles. Although Debbie says she is beginning to feel disoriented, we, too, are rejuvenated, and we see them off for McCoy's Landing in high spirits.

The mandatory holds are much closer together now, only eight miles to McCoy's Landing by the Shenandoah River. It was the first hold and vet check this morning, but pit crews were not allowed in then. At our last stop, Pickett Springs, the riders were given flashlights to help them over the infamous Sherman's Gap, and it is quite dark when we reach the broad plain that is McCoy's Landing. Generator-powered floodlights light the plain and shimmer on the Shenandoah, where two glowing floats mark a crossing for the horses.

This is the 88 mile point. There is a final vet check and 15-minute hold at Land's Run, but pit crews are not permitted there and we will intercept Debbie and Squirt at a highway crossing. If they pass the vets at McCoy's Landing. If they get to McCoy's landing.

We stare with burning eyes into the black hole at the end of the field, but no horses come in for a very long time. Al is worried--he drinks no beer and tells no jokes. A great black wall of trees twinkling with millions of fireflies hides the river, and the aromatic smell of the freshly mown field stings my nose and eyes. No one knows what grows in the field, so I put some of the five-lobed leaves in my pocket, a memento to look up later.

At last, three bobbing flashlights. There's a grey, but it's not ours. The pit crew next to us springs into action, and the rider comes to rest in a folding chair. Her face is crumpled in pain--perhaps she has been hurt--and she begins to weep as she talks to her husband:

"It was Sherman's Gap," she says. "I couldn't see anything and he was slipping and sliding coming down the mountain. I was so frightened," she says, sitting stiff and apart, with her head bowed. "I thought that I had killed my horse. I have never been so afraid."

I steal a glance at Pat and Al. They didn't hear. The damp,

pervasive cold muffles sounds. I put my third layer of clothing back on and find the sweatshirt Debbie shed early this morning; she will be cold in her thin cotton shirt when she gets here. If she gets here. How would they get an injured horse and rider off Sherman's Gap?

We pass from quiet despair to numb resignation before they come into McCoy's Landing. Not sweating, not lame, but not right either; moving automatically in disoriented fatigue. Squirt's eyes are wide and traumatized, his pulse and respiration erratic. He refuses food and only wets his mouth with the water.

"We were okay on Sherman's Gap," Debbie says, "I walked part of it with him. But I'm very disoriented, I am falling asleep in the saddle."

While water heats on the gas stove for instant coffee, I take apples and granola bars to Debbie, then offer an apple to the still unresponsive gelding. A small miracle: he accepts it, then another, and Pat looks up from her stethoscope and watch to nod approval. He's coming around. He begins to relax, to walk hesitantly, then freely. When his fluctuating pulse rate settles to a steady 56, Pat and Al learn they must bring him to the floodlights for his P & R check.

All the trauma of the dark mountain crossing returns with the noise of the generators, the blinding floodlights, and the strangers poking at him, and Squirt's pulse shoots up to 80. That can mean an extra ten minute hold, but the understanding P & R team gives Pat and Al a few minutes to calm the horse, then they recheck him away from the excitement.

Debbie and Squirt set off unsteadily for the last stop before the finish line, the 15-minute hold and vet check at Lands Run where pit crews are not permitted. But when we intercept them at a crossroads a mile and a half from Lands Run, they've passed several horses, moving along optimistically at a strong, steady trot.

Taking on our team's latest condition like three chameleons, we head for base camp to relax for a couple of hours before they come in for the final vet check. Pat heads for a twenty-minute nap, Al goes to find the finish line, and I visit the control center for an update on other riders. Radio communications from the last two vet stops report two calls for pit crews to bring trailers and retrieve horses and riders, including a middle-aged couple whose company Debbie enjoyed on the way to Pickett Springs. Reassured to learn that calls to pit crews can be heard all over the base, I join Al at the finish line.

Several two-legged marathon runners wait there for friends, and greet each arrival with cheers and hugs. I quickly learn to differentiate the distant bobbing lights of human runners from the swinging lights held by riders. The human and equine competitors who have made it to the finish seem in remarkably good shape. Al falls asleep sitting on an overturned bucket.

Two 55-mile horses hang over a paddock fence, tiredly watching the small crowd, the sporadic return of the competitors, and the single P & R team and veterinarian, Sally Ralston, left at the finish. Watching us watch the last black hole. One goes off to pick at hay and the other, a bay Arabian, lies down next to the fence to watch and yawn and doze. To pass the time, I climb the fence, sit down next to him and talk to him:

"Do you know what you're doing, horse?" I ask him. "You've gone 55 miles and you didn't even deliver the mail or pick up a gallon of milk. And here you are, right back where you started. I hope you brought home the bacon."

The horse nods sleepy agreement, pleased to have company and a nice rub. He's just what I need: large, warm, soft and friendly. If I knew him better, I would curl up with him.

Pat joins us and Al wakes with a start. It's 3:30 a.m.

"How long can it take them to do four and a half miles?" Al asks.

Arabel and Webb Coleman come in, stiff and spent and victorious, followed by the 22-year-old Appaloosa and Heather Hoyns. Louis Rukeyser arrives to wait for Alexandra. When we have resigned ourselves to an accident on the trail at this late hour, or at best to a disqualification for overtime, Debbie and Squirt amble in.

"Where have you been!" Al's concern comes out as a reproach.

"Oh," Debbie says, cheerfully, "he'd been carrying me all day, so I walked the last four and a half miles alongside him."

Squirt is a little stiff, but alert and moving willingly, and his pulse rate is a remarkable 40. Debbie does not want to keep him up another hour to try to qualify for a best condition award; she only wants to have him vetted and put him to bed.

Crossing the stableyard after bedding Squirt down, we find Alexandra Rukeyser having her mare's final vet check.

"Alexandra! You made it!" Debbie cries, hugging her, and Alexandra lights up with the first smile of a long day and night, a smile of pure delight.

Driving back to North Carolina later that morning, I remember the pungent leaves I picked in the dark of McCoy's Landing, stop, and climb over the tailgate of the pickup truck to search the pockets of my smelly jeans. The leaves have turned to dust. Even the aroma is gone. No matter. I have a memento: *To finish is to win.*

A NEST OF COTTONHEADS

Down a dirt trail that took up where my street ended, I found a nest of cottonheads. They were called cottonheads because of the children's hair, so light it was like silver. The term "cottonhead" was most often used with other adjectives, as in "a houseful of little snot-nosed cottonheaded bastards." On the other hand, my third grade teacher, who was also the principal's wife and plainly detested me, had identically colored hair, only very tightly curled, and nobody talked about her the way they did about the cottonheads. Perhaps it was because Mr and Mrs. Stuckey were pinched and scrawny and scrubbed raw, whereas the cottonheads were soft and pudgy and grimy.

The hair of my cottonheads--they were "my cottonheads" because I had discovered them--was fine and straight, and their scalps showed through, covered with a fine grit like coal dust. My cottonheads wore ill-fitting clothes, coated with the same fine grey dust even on the days they changed clothes. Their clothes and their hair created a uniformly shapeless image of grey and silver. They were barefoot, but so were many other children at school.

Marie said, "Yo' mama will kill us bof if she catches you goin' down there," but I knew Marie would not tell on me. I could not stay away from the cottonhead children. They had little to say to me, but they seemed glad to see me, and there was a humility--a word I did not know then--about them that both intrigued and worried me. When their mother appeared at the door of the shack with a fat, grimy silver-haired baby slung on her hip, I knew that while she didn't have much use for me, she wouldn't slice me up with her tongue like Mrs. Stuckey did.

One of the cottonhead girls was in my class. Her name was Elizabeth, an elegant name, like a queen's. I soon realized that she rarely brought any lunch, and when she did it was not like any food I had ever seen. Marie said that was not *my* problem, but it was. Sometimes I split my lunch with Elizabeth, if she did not vanish as soon as the lunch bell rang, and if I could get her to take it. If I ate part of my lunch while she watched, then pretended I had a stomach ache and couldn't eat any more, she would accept the rest.

There was a big fuss at school about Thanksgiving, about Pilgrims and Indians sitting down together--one time, anyway, and sharing a feast. We colored and cut out Pilgrims and Indians, live turkeys and roasted turkeys, pumpkins and pumpkin pies, corn and apples, and stuck them all over the windows and walls. We practiced a Thanksgiving play in which we prayed and gave thanks for an exceedingly long time. I was a Pilgrim. Elizabeth stood in the back row wearing an Indian headband with a feather stuck in it and watched us Pilgrims and Indian chiefs pray and eat.

All the coloring and cutting and praying and pageantry was so tiresome that I thought about other things even more than usual, like what my father said about the pageant:

"I don't know what they're giving thanks about. Nobody here ever had enough of anything except blueberries and hookworm."

One of the things I thought about was my cottonheads, and the day we were turned out for Thanksgiving holidays, my best friend Roslyn and I went straight to the grocer's. The grocery store was narrow and dark, with two long aisles leading to a refrigerated case at the back and shelves along the sides stacked all the way to the ceiling. Groceries could be charged in those innocent days, as well as delivered. I had discovered that charging things to my parents went unnoticed, but I suspected that ordering delivery might be going too far.

Roslyn and I filled two boxes with a ham, fatback, a pumpkin, sweet potatoes and white potatoes, bread, apples, cans of peas and corn. I added a sack of grits, which I had learned was the congealed white stuff in Elizabeth's lunch sack, then we struggled giddily home and hid the boxes in my garage. Marie rolled her eyes up to heaven but said nothing; she knew what she ought not to know.

Fearful that the cottonheads' mother, like Elizabeth, might not accept the food, I waited until all the houses on our street were dark before I wrestled the boxes down the road, one at a time, and eased them silently onto the cottonheads' dark porch.

Then I began to plan my cottonheads' Christmas, which ought to be more than food. Playing with Elizabeth on her porch, I sized up the tow-headed children to see who would fit my clothes and my little brother's. My mother, who had a reputation for style, had two closets full of clothes; she wouldn't miss a few. No point in looking through my father's wardrobe--he would miss even a handkerchief--but there was a sizeable "rag bag" of clothes which my mother gave to the poor when it became full. Roslyn promised clothes and she had toys to spare. I was glad to give away some like-new dolls, but I had no other toys, only books that I agonized over for days before parting with half of them for the cottonhead's Christmas.

When I came home from school a week before Christmas vacation, Marie's averted eyes and tightly pursed mouth warned that I was in deep trouble. My mother snatched up my little brother and handed him to Marie to get him out of the way before she lit into me. Her first words sealed my lips:

"Someone's going to pay for this," she hissed, shoving a piece of paper against my face and rubbing my nose in it. "Look at this!" she shouted. "What's the meaning of this?"

She held the paper before my eyes with both hands so I

could see plainly that it was the grocer's bill and that I could not explain the meaning of it. I began to bawl--sometimes bawling would circumvent what was coming next--but she grabbed me by the nape of the neck and pushed me into the hall closet.

"You can sit there and think about what you've done until your father comes home. He'll get the truth out of you."

Being too old to scream about my fear of the dark and beg to be let out, I waited, making up implausible lies and discarding them. At the end of a few hours, I could see that I would have to tell the truth, or at least part of it.

My father's first approach was politic. "You've got yourself in a mess of trouble, haven't you," he said, smiling with that dreaded glint in his eye that canceled the smile. "Want to tell me about it?"

Touched by this reasonable approach, I began to cry in earnest. "I gave the food to some poor people for Thanksgiving."

My father's smile twisted downwards in a most peculiar way for a smile to go. "I make the decisions about who is poorer than we are and who deserves to be helped. Who are they?"

"I don't know their names."

"Where do they live?"

"I don't know."

"Don't lie to me. That food has to be paid for; there's a depression on. You can't go around giving hand-outs to every poor white trash that comes whining to the door. Who are they?" I sat silent and miserable.

"I'll see if I can't refresh your memory."

I lay face down across my bed, hiked up my skirt and pulled down my panties, so filled with shame and hatred for my father that I would not cry again if he killed me. That was a mistake, refusing to cry, because once he began whipping me he could not stop until he got some kind of satisfaction. It took him so long to take his belt off that it was almost a relief when he hit me. After every three or four hits, he would stop, panting, and demand,

"Had enough?"

"Yes," I said, but I would not say anything else, and he kept on until I lost count.

Roslyn and I finished the cottonheads' gift boxes two days before Christmas, although she didn't think it was much fun after I'd been caught. I felt wonderfully Christmasey because we had collected enough from other kids--without having to say who it was for--to make up the shortfall from not being able to charge anything. What made it even more festive was Roslyn being allowed to spend the night with me, which was so rare and unexpected that we were extraordinarily good and polite and quiet. Until midnight. Then we slipped down the road to the cottonhead nest with our bounty.

The front door standing open gave us a terrible fright. Roslyn dropped her box and would have run away if I had not caught her skirt and hauled her back. Fingers of moonlight reached across the floor inside the shack without touching any sign of life, and when our fear subsided we crept onto the porch, listened, and tiptoed inside. Both rooms of the shack were empty and swept clean. The woodstove was cold, and the bucket had been cut from the well windlass on the porch.

I don't remember all the cottonhead children or even how many lived there, but I still see the faces of Elizabeth, her mother and the drooling baby, and one of the quick, belligerent little boys who was in the same class as Elizabeth and me. And although I only saw him once or twice, I still see their father. I cannot quite make out his face, but I can describe him: gaunt, a word I did not know then, and angry, a word I knew well.

BERNIE

My first look at my first foster child brings second thoughts. He is over six feet tall, and no sapling. It will take every penny of the foster parent's stipend to feed him, and why should I believe that he is harmless?

During foster parent training, it came out that the authorities did not always disclose the full facts about these children. I have been told that Bernie is mildly retarded and he molested little boys. His counselor says that Bernie is not gay; that he molested little boys because nothing else was available to him. Is this the truth? What else should I have been told?

My thoughts are reflected in the juvenile officer's face. Bernie hangs his head, looking miserably out of place and sorry to be here.

In six months, when Bernie turns 18, he will be out of the hands of juvenile authorities, tried as an adult for future offenses and sentenced to adult prisons. He has been in institutions for various reasons since he was three or four years old; comments about his history flash through my mind:

"Abused and neglected," said the state.

"We can't do nothin' with him," said the parents who abused and neglected him.

"Take him back," said his last foster parents.

That leaves me, inexperienced and apprehensive, at the end of the road for Bernie.

"Welcome to our farm, Bernie. Do you like horses?"

With a quaver and an uncertain look, he swears that he loves horses. I take him upstairs to his first room of his own and help him unpack two worn pairs of jeans, three shirts and sweatshirts, and almost enough new underwear and socks for a week. Everything he owns hardly fills two dresser drawers.

Bernie is depressed and uncommunicative for several days, but we have no time for circling each other like strange cats. The state expects me to teach Bernie how to work on a farm so he can support himself. He also must learn to take care of himself like any other seventeen-year-old, and he must understand that he can never molest another child. Having no idea how to accomplish all this, I study Bernie for clues to where to begin.

Bernie is dangerously uncoordinated, and practically blind without the thick-lensed glasses he doesn't want to wear-- because of vanity, so I know his appearance is important to him. It quickly becomes apparent that his personal hygiene has consisted of marching to the showers with the other boys- -when ordered there--and he is astonished at all the things I expect him to do for himself: wash up before meals, brush your teeth, take care of your clothes, clean your nails, this is called deodorant...the list of his new accomplishments grows longer each day. He remembers to do these personal chores if I add them one at a time, then he proudly reports that he just brushed his teeth or put his laundry away or whatever he was supposed to do.

One morning I find him at the kitchen stove when I come back from feeding the horses.

"Your coffee will be hot in a minute, mom," he says proudly. On the stove, unlighted gas hisses around the coffee pot. Bernie may blow us up or burn us down before he learns some 8-year-old living skills.

A large, marginally profitable breeding farm provides endless opportunities to learn manual skills so that Bernie can work somewhere, maybe on another farm where he can be sheltered until he is on better terms with life in the world outside of institutions. Ancient farmhouses and barns *want* things: a nail here, a window pane there, another rotted board replaced, storm windows up, storm windows down. The garden *wants* things. Then there are fences to build or mend, stalls to muck out, manure piles to load and spread with the tractors, pastures to mow or nourish.

Our resident population of 30-odd horses includes two stallions, several pregnant mares, and a bunch of rowdy young horses, all of them sent out to various pastures after morning feed and brought into their stalls at night--simple procedures that can turn into stampeding, kicking riots. Tons of water and hay and feed are toted to the horses daily. The horses are dewormed, vaccinated, groomed, trained, bred in season and, with luck, delivered of the consequences 355 days later..

Spring brings visiting mares to be bred, foal births to attend, and injured horses from the track for rest and therapy. Farm income and population doubles and farm work quadruples.

Bernie must learn self-control and patience around these large, emotional and fragile animals. There are rules about closing gates, leading horses safely, and hundreds of caveats that guard against accidents and injuries to horses and people. He earns some scary bruises before he understands that he is not the innocent victim, but the cause of the accident; then safe behavior on the farm becomes a habit to him.

Other farm work is harder for Bernie. Teaching him to drive a tractor is hopeless--too many things to do with one's hands and feet at once on an expensive, dangerous machine. He can't hit a nail until I demonstrate by driving nails left-handed, as he does; then he won't hit a nail hard enough to drive it in. He taps nails gently, respectfully--too institutionalized to swing hard at anything? No anger in there? Only fear?

Fear is the key to the offense that will put this great infant into an adult prison. Bernie is not afraid of pain, or of social censure although he is affectionate and wants to be involved with whatever is going on. His only, all-consuming fear is of being locked up again. During meals--the only time when I can count on his undivided attention--we talk about sex: wrong sex, right sex, and the consequences of both. I teach survival, not morality.

"No more little boys, Bernie. Bernie, do you know that I wouldn't lie to you?"

"Yes, mom." He smiles because it makes him happy to know I wouldn't lie to him.

"They will lock you up forever. With men who will hurt you. I don't want you to be locked up and hurt. Molesting little boys is the only thing they (always "they") won't forgive." This is a lie: I know that Bernie could easily be led into other crimes by someone else, but I can only try to fix the one thing that has everybody ready to lock him up in the place that will change him forever, the prison where adult men wait for a compliant, retarded boy.

"What in the world do you talk about with him?" my friends ask curiously.

"Sex," I say, and they laugh merrily, thinking I jest.

After several weeks of guiding, coaxing and bullying Bernie into my world, I decide that he's not as retarded as the juvenile officers described. I postulate that he missed every opportunity to learn the skills most children acquire at home, and that lack, coupled with moderate retardation, physical incoordination, and poor vision, made it easy to write him off as hopelessly slow.

Breeding and foaling is the hardest work of the year, but the season has a rhythm of hope and urgency and fulfillment that is quite beautiful. We are caught up in the rhythm, and it brings a joy to our work that eases the pain and fatigue from hard physical labor and long hours. Bernie begs to be allowed to stay up and help when the mares foal, but it's likely to be midnight and I'll be up a couple of hours after that until I'm sure everything is all right. I don't have any extra stamina for channeling Bernie's excited impulses half the night, or being distracted by him, and I refuse his requests for a long time. Then a tough, self-confident mare who's not likely to be distracted by Bernie is going to foal, and I send someone to awaken him and bring him to the barn.

Bernie is impossible; he can't stop moving around and talking. His excitement makes the mare nervous and apprehensive, and I tell him, "Be quiet and still, or go back to bed. You don't get another chance."

I begin to explain what is happening, what I do and why I do it, as if I were tutoring a visiting mare owner. I talk quietly, and he listens and watches as if he understands every word. The three of us, my mare and Bernie and me, become peaceful and go on with our business. He fetches things: a tail wrap for the mare; then clean dry towels, and I let him gently rub the wet, steaming foal; then he brings fresh water and hay for the mare. Finally, the foal is on its feet and nursing, the placenta delivered and examined and taken away, the stall cleaned and freshly bedded, and I realize that I have been talking nonstop to Bernie and the mare and the new foal for two hours.

We have progressed so far that I can go to town without taking Bernie along. Entranced with his new skills and new freedom, he no longer minds missing the trip. When I return one afternoon, my neighbor across the road phones:

"I want to tell you what a good job Bernie did this afternoon, and how much I appreciate his helping me out. I was so upset, I didn't know what to do."

My heart sinks...Bernie left the farm...what did he get into?

My neighbor says that her pony mare foaled in the middle of the day out in the pasture. Animal husbandry is not my neighbor's forte; indeed, she did not know that the recently-acquired pony was pregnant. When she telephoned for me, Bernie went to help her.

"Bernie!" I bellow, and he gallops downstairs wearing a grin so big he almost trips over it. "What happened?"

It was the little mare's first foal, and Bernie found her very agitated, standing over the tiny form in the hot sun. He picked up the foal--"the right way, mom," he assures me, carried it across the field and into a stall, and the mare followed. He fetched water and hay, bedded the stall with clean straw, and stayed with the mare until the new filly was on her feet and nursing. Then he returned to the field, plopped the placenta into a bucket, and set it on my back porch to be inspected.

I can't believe that he remembered to do all the things that he had watched only once. We go to my neighbor's, "to see how they are doing," I tell him, where I find everything in perfect order.

Returning again from town a few days later, I find a note on the door: "gon to toun." After a moment of panic, I am furious: whose writing is this, and *what* are they *doing?* I don't even know where to start looking for Bernie. Before I give in to panic and call the police, Bernie is brought home by a mildly retarded neighbor boy who has a driver's license.

"Petey, why didn't you put your name on this?" I demand, shaking the note under his nose. "I was really worried--Bernie's not allowed to go off with you or anybody else. I didn't know where he was or who he was with."

"I didn't write it," Petey says. "Bernie wrote it."

"I don't know how to spell Petey," Bernie says, "or I would of wrote his name down."

It had not occurred to me that Bernie could write. Little had been said about his educational prowess...something about a third grade level and no chance of any more education except training as a laborer. I should have guessed: I'd given him his weekly allowance, taken him to spend it and made him count out the sums and change. I saw a door opening, a sliver of light for Bernie. If he could write, he could read...something, follow simple orders, find his way...somewhere.

I send Petey home, sit Bernie down with a soft drink, and ask him where he learned to read and write. In one of the boys' homes (he wasn't sure which), a teacher (whose name he had forgotten) used to keep him after class and help him. He thought it was after his last trip home when he was eight years old, and his father--or stepfather, he wasn't sure which--broke his arm with a 2 x 4, then put him and his brother down in an empty well for a couple of days. He tells me about it matter-of-factly, showing me a deformed lump on the bone: "the doctor said it wasn't set right." Being able to read was only incidental to Bernie, neither more nor less than having his arm broken.

Down a well. In a closet. Why aren't more of us murderers?

While I ponder the amazing person who taught Bernie to read and write and do simple math, and how I might use these skills to make him self-sufficient, Bernie asks me to phone Petey so he can talk to him.

"No way," I say flatly. "You're grounded." Then--"Wait! Yes," I tell him, "you can dial Petey yourself."

"I don't know his number."

"Look it up."

"How do I do that?"

"In the phone book, here. You have to know his last name. Where he lives. His parents' names if he doesn't have his own phone." I know Petey's last name and Bernie knows the alphabet, and we find the number together.

"How do I dial?" Bernie asks.

Reading was the key to saving Bernie. There would be no more gratuitous information or services for him, only short notes or instructions for learning to do all the things most third-graders take for granted. Read the cooking instructions on the cans and packages; read the knobs on the stove--it's okay to burn it or to go hungry, but fixing it yourself is the only way you are going to eat. Spell out the times, the shows and the channels in the television guide, because the television will never be turned on again unless you know what you're going to watch. Read the feeding list, measure the horses' feed and know what each kind of feed is. And now tell me why they must have fresh water and why you must know how much they drink each day.

When the first supervised Bernie-feeding of 30 horses takes two hours, I decide to give up that project. Slipping out alone to feed next time, I find the correct amounts of feed already in each feed tub and fresh water all around--Bernie's phenomenal memory has gotten him through again.

When Bernie turned eighteen, we gave him a birthday party. He said he never had a birthday before.

He stayed on a few more months, until the state found him a job with Goodwill Industries, where he learned to drive a truck and read a map so he could collect donations from all over the county. Bernie called home often for several months, then his calls became infrequent. Almost a year later, he drove up the lane one evening, knocked on the door, and proudly introduced me to the reason he didn't need to call me anymore: his girl friend and her mother. He was living with them. I welcomed them warmly, with great relief, shouting in my heart, "Oh, Bernie, you've made it."

I wonder sometimes about the person who taught a retarded little boy to read and write and do simple math. Without that person, Bernie would have remained a frightened--and frightening--large child, to be locked up one day in an adult prison where he would abuse the weak and be abused by the strong. I was only lucky enough to discover that he was literate and realize what it meant, for I could not have taught him in the short time we had together.

Will Bernie read this? I think not. Being able to read was Bernie's ticket to the world outside institutions: he would be able to find a friend in the phone book, to follow directions, to work and take care of himself; ultimately, even, to find love. That was enough reading for Bernie: it was the gift of life.

A SUMMER WITHOUT A BEACH

Most of the summers when I was very young were spent in isolated cottages on beaches populated largely by the snakes and lizards and birds that could survive in the sparse vegetation of the dunes. Sea oats grew there, and sandspurs baked as hard and sharp as needles by the hot sand, and rattlesnakes were said to inhabit the thick tangle of wild morning glories covering the first dunes I had to cross to reach the Gulf. I marveled that rattlesnakes could live in the searing sand with no water and no food except birds and lizards that were quicker than the wind; I wondered if the rubbery eggs I found in the dunes were baked rattlesnake eggs. The beach was alive, a palpable wild and lonely thing that resented the laughter and shouts from the cottages where my parents and their friends partied, but did not mind my fascinated probing into its secrets.

The summer when my brother was six months old, however, my mother took him to a more sociable beach closer to town for a month's rest and relaxation with her friends. She left me behind, she said, "because I can't rest with you around." Marie came to live in and look after me, my father came home for dinner most nights, and everyone else went away to the beach or the mountains.

As soon as my mother's car turned the corner onto the highway to the coast and disappeared, I picked out a black and tan puppy from a neighbor's litter and smuggled it home to our garage. Longing for the beach, I sat in the oil-soaked sand and held the puppy to my heart, until it began to wiggle and lick my face and whimper; then I brought it water, played with it, cuddled it and gave it a name: Blackie, short for Black Beauty even though it would never become a horse. Next summer, I would take Blackie to the beach and teach her to swim.

When I left the puppy to answer Marie's call to supper, I learned the futility of trying to conceal crimes of the heart. Blackie's howls were heard in the furthermost reaches of a house tightly shuttered and curtained to keep out the June heat, perhaps heard all the way to the beach.

My father said it looked like a pretty sorry dog and he doubted that my mother would let me keep it; he wouldn't have a mutt like that himself. Marie said I would be the death of her, then she helped me fix a box for the puppy and saved scraps for it every day.

It was a tolerable summer. Marie told wonderful stories and jokes when no adults were about. Blackie's unquestioning love and enthusiastic complicity in whatever adventures I could conjure up were immensely satisfying; and while my friends might be gone, none of them had a dog. Feeding inedible animals was not a priority during the Depression.

My mother stayed on at the beach. When she returned, it was almost time for school to start and the baby was crawling and standing up. He was still "such a good baby" when he came home, but a number of adjustments had to be made. Life in the frame cottages at the beach was casual, primitive by genteel Southern standards. Sand on the cottage floor, in the sheets and in the food was an integral part of beach life, along with drinking water that smelled like rotten eggs. The four ladies--always a foursome to make up a bridge game, although some rotated in and out during the summer--avoided domestic chores by splitting the cost of a maid, for whom the beach developer had provided a room, toilet and shower stall downstairs. Downstairs was the street side, where long flights of wooden steps led up to cottages supported on stilts at the back and on tall dunes in front.

A boardwalk led past the screened front porches of the cottages to the snack bar, jukebox and slot machines at the beach casino. In the other direction, I could walk for hours in beauty that few recognized then and none can see now, never seeing another cottage or person. The ladies walked that way at dawn to catch crabs or gather periwinkles for stew. At twilight, they went to town to the restaurants and casinos. Although gambling was illegal, it was quite respectable and profitable almost year round--when the grand jury convened for a week, the casinos closed out of respect.

Rotating the baby through the laps of four ladies and a maid in a cottage without any china or crystal to break ended when my mother came home. In the process of rearranging her household treasures and Marie's time to accommodate an active baby, my mother hardly noticed Blackie in the back yard. Not until the next spring, when she began to garden, did my mother complain about the dog. By then, Blackie had learned a trick or two: in the presence of white adults, she crawled humbly on her belly like a snake and showed all of her teeth in a ghastly, ingratiating smile.

Blackie kept getting fatter and my father complained about "that lazy, flea-bitten mutt eating so much." But I had become wise enough to know that girl dogs had puppies, if not wise enough to know why the neighbor encouraged me to take the only female in the litter. I had reread many times the little book that had appeared when I asked were babies came from, and I was sure Blackie was going to have puppies. Each night, I dropped part of my supper into my napkin and smuggled it out to her, but each day she ate less and slept more. At first light each morning, I inspected the ballooning belly and wondered when the puppies could come. I felt carefully for individual lumps, trying to count the adorable, snuffly pups that would soon be mine.

Some mornings it was hard to wake up, because I read late into the night with a flashlight under the covers. I must have turned off the alarm in my sleep that morning, because when I woke the sun was high and I could smell bacon frying. Jolted awake by fear that I might have missed the birth of the puppies, I rushed to the window. Blackie lay by her uneaten supper near the water faucet, with her back to the house. She was very still and her belly looked twice as big. It would be today, she was having the puppies right now, that's why she didn't eat her supper.

Halfway to Blackie, I knew, but I could not stop walking towards her. I had to see the blind eyes and the taut distended belly full of worms and God knows what else, but not of adorable snuffly puppies and dreams. So this was what death looked like.

Marie came out, her twisted and scarred face sad, and put her arms around me. Together, we wrapped the ugly body in an old towel, and Marie dug a hole in the sand behind the garage. I couldn't find any sticks to make a cross, so I took apart a little boat and an airplane that I had built of wood scraps. It was an odd, clumsy cross, airplane wings and the mast of a sailboat, and as I tapped it into the ground I wondered if God would mind.

THE HUNTER'S BOUNTY

A hunter waits in my woods on a fine transitional morning between summer and fall. Within his range are my neighbors, rarely visible until the leaves fall from the wooded buffers between us. Behind me, old Garland Chambers cannot keep still: the gnarled black hands that nursed his dying wife until this spring putter compulsively about his pristine grounds. Through the woods to the west, four boys with a basketball imitate the Harlem Globetrotters; across the road from them lives a very old and reclusive couple. Across the road a dozen calves graze almost hidden by tall weeds; beyond their pasture three generations live in a large new house. From the east, a young couple and their two-year-old stroll out in good weather; on the several acres behind them my Lumbee Indian friends have a trailer, a barn, and a menagerie of children, dogs, donkeys, horses, cows and pigs. Because of my neighbors and the incidental illegality of his presence in my small woods, I did not expect the hunter.

The little girls slosh through the spring, soaking their boots and sneakers before I can show them how to cross by stepping from a half-submerged log to a tuft of moss to a squashed, thickly-woven briar bush. Their mother and I cross the spring cautiously while the girls dance up the trail.

"Slow down," I call. "If you're going to walk in the woods you have to look where you put your feet."

The   dark-eyed,   rosy-skinned   children   dart   like

92

hummingbirds from discovery to discovery . They are proudly Italian-American, an engaging combination of youth and dignity--I call them my "little Italian princesses." Their parents want to buy my farm, partly because one daughter has developed a heart ailment, partly because it is a small, rather shabby Eden that pleases the eye and gentles the spirit.

It's the little girls who *really* crave my farm. On this Sunday visit, they bring names for three half-grown cats I promised to leave for them, lavish love on astonished and intrigued horses, and spray questions like machine gun fire:

"Which is my room?" (The tree house, I say.)

"Why can't we ride all the horses?" (These are too young, that one is too heavy in foal.)

"Can we sleep in the hayloft?" (Ask your mother.)

"Will you leave Magic for us?" (Oh no, I could never leave Magic!)

Everyone thinks her name is Magic, but it's really Majik Rainmaker because her sire was Champion Majik something-or-other and she was just a scared rainmaking puppy when I got her, hardly a double-handful. Now she's big for a female, but long and graceful, with huge ears and feet and a lively interest in everything.

Hearing her name, Magic bounds back down the trail to give each little girl a quick wash with her big tongue and a thump with her long tail, then she's off to explore the edge of the woods again. Magic knows every inch of the woods and marsh that form the eastern boundary of my land. When I leave for work, she goes to the woods alone, and who knows what she does there? Flushes birds--she has a personal vendetta against every one of the thousands of birds that live here. Chases mice and rabbits--and lets them go if she catches them. Lies down in the spring and comes home covered with mud and happiness. If she has a fault, it is her love of the marsh and woods.

Perhaps being humble is a fault, too; she makes me feel guilty when she is so humble and eager to please. She tries to be a bird dog and a hunting dog. And a herd dog, trying to put the horses into their stalls for feeding or wherever else she thinks I want them to go. Never mind that I say "go on, don't help me, Magic," and the horses ignore her or chase her, she knows that a German Shepherd herds things. And a mother dog--never mind that I circumvented that possibility, that adores babies and carries the cats around by their heads and washes them. And Magic is a cross between a guard dog and a seeing eye dog: she walks with me so closely that she rubs my knee and we look like a three-legged race. She comes to fetch me when its time for chores, wakes me up before the alarm goes off, and pushes me away from things she thinks I ought not to do. When I watch television or write, she has a disconcerting habit of sitting down before me, plopping a great paw upon my knee, and staring earnestly at me with her clear amber eyes.

The sun is low when we come out of the woods. We pick cobwebs and leaves out of the girls' long hair and talk, then watch them throw a yellow tennis ball for Magic.

When Magic was young and foolish, she raided my bucket of tennis balls every day and scattered them in every room. Now that she's three years old, she has more important things to do, but she likes to play ball with children, and join any foolishness they contrive. When grandchildren visit, she sleeps on the tiny landing at the top of the stairs, just outside their room, and mopes when they leave.

One day, she spotted half a dozen young black children coming down the road on a Sunday walk with their mothers and ran to greet them. The children turned and ran screaming down the highway, their mothers and Magic after them, then me, sprinting to catch up. I caught Magic (who was delighted that these lovely chocolate-colored kids wanted to run and play), and delivered a lecture about never, never, never running away from dogs. Then, with the children clinging fearfully to their mothers, Magic and I walked them down the road to the barn to see the horses.

Twilight comes and everyone--me, Magic, five horses, three cats, two little girls, and Jeanette who still looks like a little girl--is hugged and they are gone. The weekend is gone. Magic and I do our three-legged walk to the barn, where she waits patiently while I feed horses and fill water buckets. Night has fallen when we return to our dark house. My dog usually sleeps next to my bed, where I step on her or trip over her when I get up at night, but lately she has taken to sleeping upstairs, where she still seems to hear every sound in the night. I suppose I ought to see what she's doing up there. Later.

On Monday I decide to buy groceries at noon instead of shopping after work. I usually go home to eat lunch and check on everything; today I indulge myself in lunch from the supermarket's deli. Fried chicken, real Southern turnip greens, real mashed potatoes covered with gravy, corn bread with butter and jam, three dollars. Beats peanut butter and jelly on stale bread--do people who live alone ever have fresh bread? I wrap the wing tip and backbone in a napkin for Magic. It's hard to resist giving her treats, although she never begs or looks reproachful when I eat my dinner. Long ago, I had another female German Shepherd who was also too proud to beg; I could leave her in the car with a sack of meat from the supermarket and she wouldn't touch it. Not that I really taught the dogs much--I think good farm dogs are born, not made, and only need to know what the parameters are.

Magic is not home when I return from work Monday. Maybe she's gone over the hill to visit the ugly brown dog that comes to do the marsh and woods with her some mornings, or she's gone into the woods after a rabbit. I whistle and wait. No matter, she will come soon.

She has not come home at horse-feeding time, and after I finish the chores I walk up and down the road and call and whistle. In a show of nonchalance, I give the chicken treat to the cats, fix myself a large drink, and read myself to sleep.

In my sleep, I think about what I will do if my dog is still missing in the morning. I awake several times during the night to go to each of the three outside doors in turn, open it and whistle and call into the dark. My calls bring only cats racing madly to the doors, then scratching on the windows and staring piteously through the panes.

A feeling of emptiness pervades the morning. With a growing sense of dread, I try to rush through the morning routine, but the horses dally over their feed, the cats jump on the kitchen countertops and knock things to the floor, and I drop everything and bumble along, angry and frustrated.

It occurs to me to check the basement. An unlikely notion, but having thought of it, I cannot rest until I look. The basement is a small room with an outside door that I leave open during the summer, and Magic likes to lie down there in the cool dust. It rained during the night, but there are no wet paw prints on the stairs. The ceiling light socket has gone bad, and in the available dim brown light, I see a dark outline in the far corner, not unlike a large dog. A trick of light and shadow, I tell myself, running upstairs for a flashlight.

Magic lies in the corner with her nose resting on her paws and her eyes closed. She looks very clean and shiny and peaceful. I touch her shoulder and a sound like a sigh comes from her, but she is cold and unresponsive. Dark blood wells from a deep gash two or three inches below her backbone on the left side of her chest. Rigor mortis had set in and is leaving. My mind registers clinical details and my heart writhes in more pain than I can bear. Then I cannot think at all.

Eventually, I realize that I have put the flashlight away and dressed for work. I can't go to work. I must take care of my dog--but she weighs 90 pounds and I cannot carry her up the stairs. I call the only person I know who is physically and mentally able to help, my Lumbee Indian friend. His wife promises he will come over as soon as he returns from delivering pine straw to Raleigh.

Images turn in my mind like the twisting of a knife blade: I realize that there is no blood on the steps leading into the basement or the dirt floor around Magic. She could have been killed in my basement. A searing rage begins behind my eyes and travels through arteries and capillaries to my very fingertips, until I am on fire with hatred that someone could invade my basement and drive steel into my gentle dog. I must will this person to return, draw him back with psychic fury and destroy him.

I call the Sheriff's office and explain to the dispatcher; she says she understands, and in a few minutes she locates a deputy who can come out.. I drink bitter coffee and try to compose myself.

The Deputy is large, pudgy young man with a round kind face. We talk, then he gets his flashlight and we go down the basement stairs together. He kneels to examine the wound in Magic, stands up and turns to me:

"She was shot by a bow hunter."

"How could a gash that big be an arrow? Where is the arrow?" I ask, uncomprehending.

"It was a big steel-tipped arrow for deer hunting," he says. "It came out the other side." He turns Magic over and shows me an exit wound on her right side, lower down. Seeing the downward trajectory of the wound, I realize that the bowman stood higher than his target and shot down at her. Shining his light about the basement, the Deputy shows me that there are no footprints except his and mine and Magic's. He turns the light on Magic again, and says sadly, "She was a beautiful dog."

Outside, in the sunlight, the Deputy explains that he is sure of the cause of the wound because he, too, is a bow hunter, and he tells me about 100-pound-draw compound bows that will send an arrow through a bulletproof vest.

"There is no knife that can make a through-and-through wound like that," he says.

"How come there's no blood anywhere?"

"It looks as though the arrow went through a lung and she flew home as fast as she could, to where she felt safe."

I can see Magic streak across the pasture and into the basement, to lay her nose on her paws, close her eyes, and die in dignity "where she felt safe," and I have to turn my crumpling face away from the Deputy.

"You need to get her out of there pretty soon. Do you have someone to help you?" I tell him a friend will help and thank him for coming. He says he's sorry, again, that he will report it to the Wildlife Officer, and he drives away.

I had thought of bow hunters as a different breed, more attuned to nature. More responsible. What could the hunter have seen in the moment before he raised his bow and released his arrow? My dog was black, not deer-colored. Did he hear only a rustle in the brush, shoot at a movement of leaves? Or did he kill Magic deliberately--there was the downward trajectory of the arrow through her side. It could have been one of the little Italian princesses pierced through and through. It could have been me--I am as tall as a deer's head and I move quietly through the woods and marsh.

What did the hunter think after he released his arrow? Did he recover his steel-tipped arrow, wipe away the blood and fragments of tissue, and keep on hunting?

Generations of hunters on both sides of my family assumed, wrongly, that I would understand and approve of them, join

LOST LAMBS & BLACK SHEEP

them if they invited me. My great-uncle Jack kept my grandmother's table supplied with game in return for his room and board and a little whiskey money. Even as a small child, this arrangement baffled me, because my widowed grandmother produced, alone, more ham, bacon, sausage, beef and chickens than she could use. The bounty of my grandmother's farm tasted infinitely better than the bloody, bedraggled scrawny lumps of fur and feathers that Uncle Jack dumped beside the sink for her to pluck, skin, eviscerate, clean and cook.

My father could have been happy as a professional Great White Hunter if that calling provided wealth and public adulation. Since it did not, politics was his profession and hunting his avocation. Whatever could be hunted, he shot. Whatever was edible was packaged for his freezers by a meat packing plant; as it accumulated freezer burn, he gave it away. He ranked his trophies by the rarity and size of the kill, the eliteness of the company in which he hunted, and the quantity of the kill. The only prize that eluded him was the lion. Glass eyes of every size and shape except leonine stared reproachfully from walls, glass cases, and entire free-standing animals in his offices, library, trophy rooms, attics and sheds. There were tigers, polar bear and brown bear, rhino, deer elk, moose, water buffalo, sheep and goats, ruminants and ungulates of every exotic breed. Of elephants, he brought back only the feet and tusks, and a recipe for elephant stew.

It is easier to think about my father and other hunters than to think about Magic. What are the sick needs and male insecurities that drive them to pursue prey that is no threat to man and no match for a gun or bow? What is manly in killing a frightened, fleeing animal that is--probably--less intelligent than the hunter? How can hunters claim to hunt only for food, when it cost hundreds of times more to put meat on the table by hunting than to buy the best commercially-produced meat?

99

The tenets of the National Rifle Association and other less-organized gun-toters are delivered with the conviction of Moses presenting the ten commandment: The deer must be killed or they will overproduce and starve; wolves, bobcats and coyotes steal lambs, chickens, and babies; wild horses eat *our* grazing lands; there are more ducks, geese, quail and pheasant than hunters can ever endanger; *we* practice conservation; *our* fees support national forests and game preserves; it is an American right to bear arms.

"It is an honorable sport," my father once said to me. "We have a President who hunted over baited fields," I replied. My father didn't see a problem with that.

If hunting is an honorable sport providing the thrill of the chase and requiring wit and cunning, then let the hunters hunt each other in an even match. The hunters could carry the purported male bonding of this "sport" to its natural conclusion: the winners could eat the loser in the ultimate "roast."

There is no way to avenge my dog's death. The Deputy, and later the Wildlife Officer, commented that the law forbids hunting on private land without written permission from the landowner, "but there are people in this area who have no respect for other people's property." They mention the Browns, sending me into a frenzy of reading mailboxes and peering into garages for hunting equipment.   But if I could find evidence to prove who killed Magic, the bow hunter's punishment would be minor, and he still would live in my neighborhood knowing that I turned him in. There are horses on my farm, helpless and mute, without a farm dog to look after them; the image of my carefree yearlings or my pregnant Thoroughbred mare, near term, pierced by an arrow, is beyond contemplation. It is better not to know the face of the hunter; if I know him I cannot rest until I get justice.

Once I was not afraid of hunters, or much of anything else.

Now I am vulnerable. Now I come home for lunch every day: 17 minutes to get home--I open my car door and Magic is not there to greet me; I check the horses--the deer-colored yearlings first; check the mail; eat standing up; 17 minutes to get back to the office. I am afraid not to come home. I hate to come home. If I had come home for lunch on Monday, would Magic have lived?

Before the bow hunter killed Magic, I never thought about my uncurtained windows. If anyone looked in, they would not know that the large dog by my side was a wimp. My home was a safe and friendly place shared with a friend: a dog with a clock in her head for the daily routine, who worried when I worried, and trusted me to take care of her as she took care of me.

There is a yellow tennis ball lying in the corner where I planted gladioli bulbs in the spring, along with Luffa squash to weave the fence and intoxicate the bees with their yellow blossoms. Spring has turned to fall and the blossoms to giant squash, and the goddamn tennis ball can lie there forever. Some mornings, the ugly brown dog waits in the pasture where the woods begin. It never comes closer, but waits patiently in its place for Magic to come out. It doesn't seem such an ugly dog now.

Two stray dogs came out of my woods today and chased the horses, then I had to run into the pasture and chase the dogs away. Magic never allowed other dogs near the horses. Soon a foal will be born, wobbly-legged and foolish and vulnerable to dogs. The animal control officer will take the stray dogs away for me--if I am here to call him when the dogs come, and if he can get here before the dogs leave. Fat chance. I may have to buy a gun I do not want and watch for the dogs and shoot them. Then I will hope that when I bury the dogs they are not wearing collars that tell me someone wants them back. It is almost as bad a world for bad dogs as for good dogs.

I must exorcise these ghosts. I go upstairs to see why Magic abandoned my bedside and slept up there lately. To the right of the landing is the room where I thought she might have curled up on the rose-colored down comforter on the bed. No, nor did she sleep in the hall leading to the attic. I always know where Magic slept, because she leaves a flattened pattern of long hairs, like a nest. On the bed in the grandchildren's room, there is a quilt with a starburst pattern made of ribbons won by my children. Long ago, my youngest daughter made the quilt by hand, slowly, and when she brought her two little boys to visit this summer, she brought the quilt to me. A kind of rite of passage, I thought. Magic has left her nest pattern on the starburst.

I take the quilt downstairs to shake it out the door and let the hair and debris float away on the wind, then put it in the washing machine. Dog hairs still cling to the carpet everywhere, drift across the kitchen floor and collect along the baseboards, waiting for the final exorcism.

I will not seek out another dog because it takes a very long time to teach a young dog all the things a farm dog must know. Because it's too hard for a young dog to be left alone every day while I am at work. Because I have put too much of myself into a good dog, and part of me has been killed.

Putting an almost-full 40-pound sack of dog food and a box of dog bones in the pickup truck, I drive to the local dumpsters to place the food in the weeds behind the bins for the skin-and-bones, shamefaced dogs that scavenge there. Then I go home to wander the pasture alone. Stooping to pull weeds now and then, I remember Magic's protesting whimper because this activity worried her, and I catch myself waiting for her to push me away from the weeds, as if she were saying "c'mon, let's not do this." I walk the woods and marsh alone, evoking a ghost.

THE INTJ BRINGS A CROWD HOME

Swinging into the long dark lane, I see that the lights have been turned on for me. We are home, all six of me reunited by five days of self awareness. *Personal Power and Influence,* the workshop was called. Self-awareness is what it was. Perfect Child is riding high, playing lookout; Rebellious Child crouching, a boxer waiting for the bell; Adaptive Child straddling the fence. Nurturing Parent has mixed liniment and rolled bandages; Critical Parent is sleeping off a psychic hangover, and Adult is just cruising. We've unloaded sixteen tons and what'll we get? We'll see.

In a satisfying symbolic touch, I leave my baggage in the pick-up and take only my cameras inside. With her empty overload baskets suspended from a pole balanced on Adaptive Child's shoulders, the INTJ can hardly squeeze us all through the door into my home. INTJ--Introspective-Intuitive-Thinking-Judging--is my newly-acquired label? diagnosis? panacea?

My fourth child sleeps in this house most of the time, eats here occasionally. She zips in and out, a bullet train between trading crude oil, exchanging strokes with clients, law school on nights and weekends; a power suit moving in the eye of a hurricane. She rests and refuels here.

Her daughter *really* lives here, part giant snail leaving a sticky trail, part poltergeist. But she's an okay kid, remarkably so for having traveled in the eye of her mother's hurricane since infancy.

I am the resident adult, which means that my daughter can fulfil her needs without fear and guilt: her 12-year-old

103

daughter will be safe from any crazies that might find their way down our rural lane; I will take her to volleyball practice, to have her braces adjusted, to tennis lessons and play rehearsals. I am neither babysitter nor cop nor ratfink (but, oh the temptation!). I hear good stuff/bad stuff that must be shared the moment my granddaughter comes home from school; I am a rehearsal hall, mute, with good acoustics.

It works for me, too. I cherish the hours alone to do my favorite work, interrupted only when earning a living becomes unavoidable. I fill a need, a comfortable role for one who was "needed" by many people for many years, and I receive the kind of love that set my children free to leave home and return without fear. Daughter, granddaughter and I pass like ships in the night, blowing our whistles and flashing our running lights in friendly recognition.

My God, the house is CLEAN. The kitchen sink is empty and the floor doesn't crunch underfoot. My mail is ON MY DESK; Critical Parent, who was counting all the places the mail might be left, says "This means something bad has happened." Perfect Child whimpers:"Maybe they don't need me, didn't miss me at all." Rebellious Child flexes her muscles.

Is that a cow patty growing mold on the dining table? It's a cake with one used candle and a note stuck in the icing:

Welcome home!

Happy Birthday!

We love you, too.

I pretended not to see my granddaughter's hurt when I didn't eat the last cake she baked, then I looked askance when she defiantly ate it all herself. Regretting that unsubtle piece of rejection, I cut a big piece of cake and wash it down with a beer--gosh, they have filled the refrigerator with beer for me. I will cut a piece every day while she is in school, and she will never know how much the dog enjoyed it. I add a bright pink note to the icing:

It's beautiful!

Thank you!

My phone messages are LEGIBLE, with DATES and TIMES. They are addressed to "Bobo," a nickname from other grandchildren, heretofore disdained as undignified by this daughter and granddaughter. There's another note:"We told everyone you wouldn't be back until day after tomorrow."

Recognizing all these small signals of caring, Perfect Child grows an inch taller.

The mail is mostly birthday cards. Adaptive Child is sad that there are no letters of acceptance from editors, glad there are no rejection slips. The card from my youngest child is fire-alarm red with a new return address, an apartment, not the home from which she ejected her husband in a trial separation last year. Nurturing Parent opens the envelope with unsteady hands. My youngest child always sends sentimental cards-- this one is humorous and contains not one word of explanation.

Seeing that the postmark is five days old, Nurturing Parent cries out, "Hang in there, the support troops are ready," and picks up the phone.

Adult puts the phone down reprovingly:"It's one o'clock in the morning in Pennsylvania."

I tiptoe past the living room, obviously just vacuumed for the benefit of Critical Parent (who is prevented from writing in the dust on table tops by a goose from Rebellious Child), and find my daughter awake.

"I was going to give you until 12:30, then call the sheriff," she tells me before we share warm fuzzies.

"Is everything all right?" Nurturing Parent is filled with apprehension.

"Everything is fine, except we missed you and it was hard to manage without you. Not enough hours. The mosquitoes have been terrible--nothing worked."

"I'll take care of it tomorrow." Critical Parent is smiling.

"We cleaned up the kitchen, picked up the living room and vacuumed tonight."

"It looks great. You didn't have to do that."

"I know. I didn't want you doing it on your first day home." All of us hug her again, and we talk and laugh until Adult reminds Perfect Child and Nurturing Parent that my daughter and the rest of us need sleep; Critical Parent is already snoring.

I awake to an empty house, a filled coffee pot, and three hungry horses staring reproachfully over the fence, ears pricked for sounds of life. When I arrive with their buckets of feed, each waits with unusual restraint at its own feed tub. After only a bite, the six-months old colt leaves his feed and comes to me.

"What's wrong," I ask anxiously, giving him Adult and Nurturing Parent's expert eye. Perfect Child knows what's wrong in a flash, puts her arms around his neck and holds him close. The colt stands like a warm statue, soaking up reassurance that he has not been abandoned by his caretaker. When I step back, he returns to his bucket and attacks his breakfast. My ancient stallion is picking at his feed morosely and looking at me out of the corner of his eye. While I hug him, my ordinarily greedy broodmare leaves her feed to stand at her gate and give me that dangerous, threatening look that has stopped large blacksmiths and veterinarians in their tracks. I know what that look really means, and I hug and stroke her until she relaxes, sighs, and turns back to her breakfast. It's nice to be missed.

While the horses eat, Perfect Child discovers that the hibiscus bean vine's lavender blossoms have become beautiful garnet red bean pods, promising seeds for spring planting, and the daisy the dog slept on has defiant new blooms on its deformed limbs. Critical Parent would pull the loufa squash vines off the okra, but for the chorus: "There will be loufa sponges to tuck in Christmas packages; we are sick of okra!"

The most recently poisoned blight-of-the-week is retreating from the azaleas and lawn--NIGYYSOB!*--and the denuded sweet-spire has produced three healthy new leaves. But the new green algae climbing half-way up the garage-apartment pushes a button, which dumps a brick into Adaptive Child's overload baskets. If I spend an hour treating that building, I ought to spend a couple more hours treating the house (two more bricks fall, causing Adaptive Child to cry out in pain), and God knows why I should have to spend time and money on dangerous chemicals to keep my house from wearing algae fur and the whole five acres from returning to primeval slime . . .

Whoa. That's not *my* algae. It must be *God's* algae, or Mother Nature's, or whoever's in charge here. If God wants to grow algae, that's *her* problem. The bricks rise from Adaptive Child's overload baskets and float away, pink sausages in the sky.

"Okay," says Rebellious Child, "but next time somebody dumps on US, *I'm* going to wipe out that algae."

*Now I've Got You, You SOB!

TO KILL A LION

Shining eyes stared from every wall, and Jeffers shook his head at an unpleasant fantasy that they had been waiting for him. It was only because he was bone tired, and sick of trudging overgrown property lines and standing in dank, unheated old mausoleums with real estate agents who wouldn't shut up long enough to find out what he was looking for.

This room was a rustic postscript stuck on the formal mansion to provide more wall space for the hunting trophies harvested by its owner. The paneling was unmarred by boisterous guests, the leather cushions bore no stretch marks. Only chair legs left their mark on the green carpet before it faded to a bilious color that clashed with the curiously ornate blue urn on the mantel of an oversized stone fireplace.

"What about all this stuff?" Jeffers asked, indicating rows of deer with their supplicant ears pricked forward and, over the mantle, a pair of tigers snarling at the large blue urn.

"It all goes with the house," answered the real estate agent. "There's some real valuable antiques here, lots of history. The owner went all over the world to hunt the game. He shot those over there," the agent said, waving at a rare species of velvet-eyed antelope, "on his last trip to Africa; told everybody they set records. 'Course he went there to kill a lion. He said that a lion was the only thing he ever wanted that he didn't get."

"They're no use to us," Jeffers said. "The furniture's reproductions, bugs have gotten into the game trophies, and nobody would want those boxes of plaques and photographs. That blue urn's not a bad piece, but I can't imagine what it could be used for."

"I don't know about that. All I know is what the widow told me on the phone, sell it all 'as is.'"

The old man turned his back on Jeffers and shuffled away, making scratchy footsteps across the brick tiles of the solarium and whispery footsteps over the polished wood of the living room. He stood in the hall at the open front door, staring reproachfully at the trickle crossing the dried-up lake bed like a tear down a wrinkled cheek.

"It's a fine piece of property," he mumbled. "They don't build 'em like this anymore. Little paint, little yard work, fix the dam and the lake'd fill up. You'd have a million dollar piece of property here."

"I don't mean to offend you," Jeffers told the back of the agent's head. "At the right price, this property does have possibilities for one of our resort campgrounds."

The agent turned quickly to face him. "We can work something out, Mr. Jeffers. Lemme buy you a drink and we can talk about it."

"I don't have much time before my plane," Jeffers said, wanting the drink, not wanting to get involved with the old man.

"No problem, sir. I've got a key to the liquor closet and we've got ice here. The widow keeps the electricity on, on account of the insurance and the alarm system--goes right to the sheriff's office, now that's a real nice feature, and Uncle Tom always kept the liquor closet well stocked. Uncle Tom, you know, is what the kids used to call him at the school they named after him. He went there ever year to give out pencils with his name on them, even when he had to make a special trip from Washington..."

"I don't think..." Jeffers began, but the agent rushed on:

"You know they built that big library for him, too--they used to call it "Uncle Tom's reading room" behind his back."

"Why don't you fix us a drink," suggested Jeffers, intrigued.

He followed the agent down the hall to the kitchen and waited while he unlocked a pantry door.

"My word," he said, seeing the unopened cases on the floor and the shelves filled with dusty bottles, "this is worth more than the furniture."

"Yessir, Uncle Tom didn't stint on some things. You should have seen his gun collection, worth a fortune. What's your pleasure?"

"Open a new Chevis, please. Why don't we sit in the dining room? At least there are no rotting heads in there."

"All right," the agent said. He filled the glasses with ice. "I hate to see things get run down like this. Uncle Tom had a lot of pride. They say that's why he stayed with his second wife so long--he never could admit he'd made a mistake. Couldn't stand to lose, either; Uncle Tom always got even."

He led Jeffers into the dining room and wiped the dust from a corner of the dark formal dining table with his sleeve before setting the bottle and glasses down. "Now you have to admit this is nice furniture in here, Mr. Jeffers."

"Yes," Jeffers replied, looking at the pictures on the wall. One was out of place among the oil paintings, a yellowed and cracked photograph of a row of solemn people with the lean, hungry faces of the post-resurrection South.Except for a splendidly dressed infant held like a scepter on his mother's lap, they wore everyday clothes, as if they had stopped work in midday and lined up for an itinerant photographer. An arrow had been pasted on the picture, pointing to the infant. His mother was fortyish, with a smooth, stern face, long pale eyes, thin lips pressed firmly down at the corners, and thick grey hair piled into a high pompadour. Beside her, a tall, rawboned man glared at the photographer through a frizzled grey thicket of hair, eyebrows and waist-length beard. The faces reminded Jeffers of the game trophies--a look of being shot at a vulnerable moment and imperfectly preserved for posterity.

"How long has this place been empty?" Jeffers asked.

The agent replenished his drink and inspected the unevenly worn heels of both his shoes before answering.

"Well, sir, the widow didn't come back here at all after he died, but it's only been empty a year. Her sister come and packed up her things for her, then lived here for a while."

"I believe I remember that there was something on the national news about his death," Jeffers mused. "What happened to him?"

"The way I heard it, his wife was off visiting her mother for a couple of weeks, and he must of died right after she left. They say he was sitting out there in that room off the kitchen where they always sat, eating lunch and watching an old John Wayne movie when she left." Looking at once pleased with himself and uncomfortable, the agent swallowed half his drink before continuing.

"When she come home, she heard the television playing and she could see through the glass in the back door that he was still sitting in that chair, and the dog was up on him. It was a nice blue tick coon dog, first dog he'd had in years. Shame they had to shoot it, wasn't the dog's fault, but after what happened nobody wanted it around. The widow didn't even open the door, just got back in her car and drove sixty miles all the way back to her sister's before she called anybody."

"No wonder you haven't sold this place."

"I've only had it listed a few weeks," the agent said. "Another company had it before. Besides, there wasn't anything wrong...I mean, they cleaned the house up like new. Heart attack, they said, been dead a couple of weeks. She had to have him cremated, which caused a lot of talk because he was dead set against cremation. Ha-ha! I didn't mean to make a joke!"

"Didn't anyone miss him in two weeks?"

"No, he was always coming and going. He'd outlived most of his friends, and she didn't like the ones that was left or his kids coming by."

Jeffers thought a little history might be good for business; they could hang the old family portrait and some of the game trophies in the lodge.

"Tell me more about Uncle Tom," he said.

"Here, let me sweeten your drink." The agent poured two fingers into Jeffers' glass and three into his own, loosened his tie, tilted his chair back on two legs, and continued:

"You know, Uncle Tom was real proud of this house. Shame he didn't build it for the first wife; she would have entertained a lot of fancy people. It always seemed like a sad kind of house to me. Oh, his daughter used to come liven it up ever now and then, but that was a long time ago when she was raising all them little kids. After her kids was grown, she come back and testified for him when he divorced Jewel, and wrote his book for him. Didn't stay but a couple of years. He got married again and the new wife wanted her gone."

"Were there any other children?"

"His son and his favorite grandson drowned in a boating accident, not long before Uncle Tom died. The other grandson hung onto the boat all night and the Coast Guard picked him up the next morning. He come down for Uncle Tom's funeral. The old man didn't have much use for him, he was a real quiet boy. Name was Daniel--they used to call him 'Daniel in the lion's den'."

"Is 'Jewel' the owner?" Jeffers interrupted.

"No sir," the agent said, shaking his head. "Let me go back a little. Jewel was Uncle Tom's second wife and they didn't have any children. The two children was from his first wife-- she left him when they was half-grown. It's his third wife that owns this house.

"You see, when he divorced Jewel he told the judge he

wanted the house for his children, for "posterity," he said. Uncle Tom loved this house more than anything in the world, except maybe hunting. He even tried to give it to the state for a historical site."

"Why didn't he leave it to his children, then?"

"I dunno," the agent said. "A lot of people wondered about that. Anyway, Uncle Tom also told the judge that Jewel drank and wouldn't go out in public with him. Being in politics, he went to ever thing that happened in this state.

"So the judge gave him the divorce and the house, and most of the other property. Week after he got the divorce, he married the third wife and changed his will to give her the house and half of the property he had left. But she never went anywhere with him either, although I don't think she drank. I've never seen her myself and I don't think but one or two people in this county ever did; she hired me over the phone. They say she looks a lot like his mother, blue eyes and black hair down to her waist. Young woman, less'n half his age."

"Where does the widow live now?"

The agent splashed whisky into his glass and onto the table, wiping the table with his sleeve and making a round swirl of wet dust before he answered.

"Since her sister died, she mostly stays over in Pensacola. That's where I sent the papers to list the property."

"The sister died? While she was living here?"

"I didn't say that," said the agent, rubbing away the damp spot on the table with his other sleeve. "Well, yes, she was living here and running the business. Maybe you saw the sign by the road, Bed and Breakfast. She quit teaching school and stayed out here alone. People said that Uncle Tom left her some money, too."

Jeffers' eyebrows made interested peaks. "She ran a bed and breakfast inn here?"

"Oh, she had a real business, but she had some problems

with it. The most popular room was the master bedroom because it had a private bath. It was a fine room then, with a king-sized lace canopy bed and lace curtains, and real polar bear and mountain sheepskin rugs on the floor. But sometimes guests left during the night and checked in at the motel in town; they claimed they heard rattling and scratching and crying out in the night. But you know, city people aren't used to country noises and the noises old houses make."

"What happened to the sister?"

"Nothing *happened* to the sister. She was a bad diabetic and she just died, laying on that lace canopy bed upstairs in the master bedroom. She was a real pretty woman, blonde hair and dark skin like those California girls you see on TV. Come to think of it, his first wife was a schoolteacher, too, and she was blonde and dark-skinned..."

"Are you sure this widow owns the property?"

"Yessir. I seen the deed." The agent chuckled. "Unless Uncle Tom still owns it. He might still be here since he didn't get that big funeral he planned on." He looked about the room anxiously. "It's getting late. My wife don't like me to be out here after dark."

He got up unsteadily and turned on the dining room chandelier, then stumbled through the house turning on all the downstairs lights except, Jeffers noted, the light in room where Uncle Tom had died watching John Wayne. When he returned to the dining room, Jeffers asked, "Not afraid of ghosts, are you?"

"I don't believe in ghosts!" the agent exclaimed, indignantly. "It gets cold and dark in here early this time of year."

"I was joking," Jeffers said, realizing that it had turned quite cold, although the ice had melted in the bowl and a greasy grey film floated on the water. "But I do believe in ghosts, friendly ones as well as malevolent ones."

The agent stood by his chair, looking uncertainly from the

almost empty bottle to the open front door where the late afternoon sun laid a warm patch on the oak floor, and back again to Jeffers.

"Get your briefcase and sit down," Jeffers said. "I want to make an offer on the property. Then you can take me to the airport. Do you want to get some more ice first?"

Picking up the bowl, the agent turned towards the kitchen, then turned back and put the bowl down. "I've had enough to drink. Do you want some ice?"

"I'll take mine neat." Jeffers wiped the grey film from the inside of his glass with his handkerchief, and refilled it.

When they finished writing the offer, Jeffers said, "Tell the widow that this is a cash offer and the only one we will make. Call me Thursday morning before ten."

"If I could tell her what you mean to do with the house, it might help." The agent's voice rose hopefully. "This is not near what the property is worth, you know."

"Worth to whom?"asked Jeffers. "Just present it. No counter-offers. She should remove the furnishings and personal property before closing; we don't want any of them."

"Mr. Jeffers? Helen said you wanted to see me."

Jeffers looked up, frowning, trying to place this particular fresh young face and the reason it seemed to be suspended, disembodied, near the top of his slightly ajar office door. A nice open face with a smattering of freckles, just enough tan to look healthy but not jockish, guileless round eyes...hell, they all looked alike nowadays.

"Oh, yes. Daniel. The Highway 90 property. Come in." The head was followed into the office by an MBA suit, which stood politely at attention while Jeffers shuffled through the files on his desk, selected one and opened it.

"That was a good lead, Daniel. We closed on that property last week. Let's see..." He began turning the pages. "Sit down, won't you?"

Daniel perched on the edge of a straight chair, leaned forward, and wedged his tightly clasped hands between his knees.

Jeffers leaned back in his chair and made a tent of his fingers. "I do not feel that the house has the right aura for a lodge."

"I don't understand, sir. I thought the mansion was the main feature of the property."

"I am not sure that I need to explain it to you. However, in the language of your generation, the house gives off bad vibrations."

"For Chri--sorry, sir. I--er--may I ask what you plan to do with the house, sir?"

"Bulldoze it," Jeffers said. "Exorcise it into a big hole in the ground. The house site is the best location for the pool. Behind the pool, trailer and RV hookups scattered through the woods. Nothing between the pool and the lake. Plenty of room on a hundred and twenty-five acres."

Daniel's face was white, freckles leaping into bold relief, and Jeffers realized that his voice had been harsh.

"Yes sir," Daniel said. "When do you want to leave?"

"I'm not going to the site," said Jeffers, "you are in charge of this one."

Color flooded back into Daniel's face. "I don't know how to thank you, Mr. Jeffers...I didn't expect to have this opportunity..."

"Thank me by doing a good job, or you will be looking for another position without references."

"I will do a good job, Mr. Jeffers. When do you want us to start?"

"As soon as you can get the demolition crew there."

"Yes sir." Daniel unclenched his tingling fingers and resisted the urge to massage them. "Is there anything else?"

"Yes. Consign the furnishings and personal property left there to an auction across the state line. No one in the company is to keep any of them. You can divide up the liquor closet with the crew, if the real estate agent didn't get it first. Be sure that the debris is hauled to the landfill--I don't want it buried on the property. Rita has the plans. She will have everything ready for you by tomorrow morning."

Daniel left with the poise becoming a project manager, shoulders straight and face expressionless, closing the door gently behind him. On the other side of the door, his chest hurt as if he had been running and his hands were wet and cold. He wondered if he had sweated through the coat of his new suit. He had sweated like this on the day his new young stepmother went off to visit her mama. He had set the drink he fixed for Grandfather on the table beside him, because his hands were shaking too much to hand it to him. He had played with the half-grown blue tick pup until Grandfather finished the drink, fixed him another, then a sandwich, adjusted the television, rumpled the pup's velvety ears in farewell, and fled. He ought to have found some way to take the pup with him; he still saw it standing on its back legs, nose pressed against the back door pane, whining anxiously after him.

He could see the blue urn, his grandfather's favorite shade of blue, on the dusty mantle in the trophy room, and the old man's ashes and bits of bone and teeth whirling like a tornado in the urn, rattling and scratching at the gold lid, fighting to reorganize, to escape to grind them all down again. The back of his neck was icy; he must have sweated through his collar, too. The words of a cousin echoed through the pounding in his head:"We'll never feel safe until we know Grandfather's gone."

As he went down the hall to his cubicle, Rita smiled up at him from her glass enclosure, squeezing her arms against her

117

sides to push her breasts forward in the way she thought excited him. The fluorescent light penetrating her glasses made her eyes huge, magnifying the little cross-hatched lines around them.

Daniel smiled back at her triumphantly, thinking that she knew Jeffers meant to bulldoze his grandfather's mansion, and she kept it from him. He had not seen that side of Rita during his careful courtship of her. He had thought he couldn't trust her because she talked too much; now he knew he couldn't trust her because she kept things from him. Because she knew that he should have been the owner of the mansion. He mentally consigned her to the mansion's landfill with the other debris of his life. As soon as the project got underway, he would have her up for one lusty, final, weekend.

PILGRIMAGE TO ATHENS

The knocking was a dream. Still, Anne half-roused to wonder: a horse kicking in the barn? No, too close. Cats on the back porch? No, too regular. Tap-tap-tap. Tap-tap-tap. The hypnotic rhythm tugged her down into warm exhausted sleep. It was only a dream. She had been full of uneasy premonitions all day, probably coming down with some bug brought by visiting grandchildren. Grandchildren! Leaning groggily on one elbow, she strained to hear the soft sounds of their sleep. The tapping was insistent and it was downstairs at the door. Perhaps her daughters had forgotten to take a key when they went out for the evening. She kicked the covers back and sat on the edge of the bed, shivering at the cold boards beneath her bare feet.

"I'm coming!" she called. Halfway down the stairs, she realized that no one had answered; not like the girls--they would shout back, joking about being locked out in the cold night. Worriedly, she scrambled back up the stairs to find slippers and a bathrobe, stumbling, fumbling in the dark, trying not to think that a policeman could be standing at her front door with news she could not bear to hear. Fastening her robe, she turned too quickly towards the hall and struck her head on the edge of the bedroom door. Bloody fool, she thought, stunned and disoriented by the sudden pain. A warm trickle was running down her cheek when she opened the door.

"Well, I was beginning to think you were dead. You must sleep very soundly--a clear conscience, no doubt." Emma James stood outside the storm door, smiling her one-sided smile and looking as if she had arrived at four o'clock tea instead of midnight. "Aren't you going to let me in?"

"Mother! What in the world--" Enormous relief at not finding a policeman at the door gave way to disbelieving shock. Anne had not seen her mother for years, never expected to see her again, even though she lived only eight hours away. It had to be a dream. But she could feel the cold air pushing through the old storm door, and she opened it and let her mother into the lighted hallway.

"I am in the area at a meeting," Emma James said. "I'm staying at a Bed and Breakfast, and I forgot my key. Tonight's session ran late and I didn't want to wake the owners, so I thought I would stop in here. Unless, of course, you don't have room for me."

"Of course there's room. Candy and Stephanie are here for the holiday, but you can have my room and I'll crawl in with the grandchildren."

"Then I'll just go to a motel, if you have a full house. I don't see as well at night as I used to, and your house was closer."

"It's no trouble. I rather like sleeping with the grandchildren, they're warm and cuddly," Anne said, thinking, 'she *is* 80, and she's not spent a night in my house nor I in hers for 25 years. She doesn't look 80 years old. She looks trim, elegant, fresh. Maybe a little frail.' Then Anne felt sorry for her mother: she *was* old and maybe she really wanted to see Anne and couldn't just say so. Anne took her coat and hung it in the closet, the buttery feel of camel hair clinging to her fingers.

"Can I make you a cup of tea, or some warm milk?"

"Oh no, you know I can't drink tea at night and milk doesn't agree with me any more."

"No, I didn't know."

"I don't suppose you have any good mineral water?"

"As a matter of fact, I have some Perrier." Anne took her mother's arm and led her down the hall to the kitchen. The arm was so thin through the woollen suit, no more than a bone. In the morning, they might talk for a little while and Anne might tell her mother what had happened to her and her children in the last few years; maybe, for once, she would tell her the bad things as well as the good ones. Then she would ask about Emma James' family, looking for clues to the way they were, Anne and her mother. Maybe, here in my own home, Anne thought, she will tell me about my ancestors, instead of talking endlessly about her travels and friends and admirers and successes and her nieces and my brother and his children. Probably not; she will ask my daughters and grandchildren about their lives, then respond with silence or stories of my nephews. No matter. It will be over in a few hours.

Anne wiped the dust off the bottle of Perrier, wondering if mineral water went bad over the years. Perhaps she ought to drink some, too. No, a scotch and soda would be more in keeping with her queasy feelings.

Later, Anne could not remember what they talked about, only that it was a friendly, almost affectionate talk, ending when she was half finished with her drink and her mother pushed away from the kitchen table and asked to be shown to her room. She took the fragile arm again, which was strange because they never touched and she could not actually remember how robust her mother's arm had felt before, and they walked together up the stairs to the long L-shaped balcony that led past the bedrooms and bathrooms.

"That's the cleanest bathroom," Anne indicated the one grandchildren were not supposed to use. "Let me get you a nightgown and I'll change the bed while you wash up."

Emma James silently appraised the bedroom, accepted the gown, went into the bathroom and closed the door. Anne swiftly changed the sheets, gathered up carelessly tossed clothes and took them away. The bathroom door remained closed. There was no sound; had she heard running water while she tidied the bedroom? She lit a cigarette and took it into the hall to wait, blowing smoke over the balcony away from the bedroom.

She went downstairs to dispose of the cigarette butt and look at the clock. Almost one o'clock. They had talked for a only few minutes, much less time than her mother had been in the bathroom--if she became ill or died here, it would be the ultimate injury. Shamed by that thought, Anne trotted briskly up the stairs and knocked on the bathroom door.

"Mother! Are you all right? Can I get you anything?"

The door opened and her mother, clad in Anne's long-sleeved, high-necked nightgown, stood in the doorway with an intense look on her face.

"I was worried; you were in there so long."

Her mother reached out her arms as if to hug her. Astonished, Anne hesitated, then stepped forward and raised her arms to return the embrace. Her mother's hands dug into her face, clawing, tearing, ripping skin and flesh.

"Oh, my God! Mother! What are you doing!" Anne cried, trying to push her away. She could not stop the matchstick arms as strong as iron bands, the hands tearing at her face. How could she be so strong? Weeping and crying out in fear and horror, Anne grasped one of the wiry arms, taking the wrist in one hand and the elbow in the other and twisting the arm, trying to make her stop. There was a terrible snap, and she held one of her mother's arms. The other arm still tore at her face. Forced against the balcony, blood streaming from her right eye, Anne broke the other arm off, and her mother fell to the floor.

Wetness trickled down her face, running warm between her breasts and icy down the back of her neck. She could not find the courage to turn on the light or to open her eyes; she could not stop the brutal, graphic images flickering in her mind.

Then she could not lie there in psychic pain any longer, and she got up and felt her way down the hall to a window where the night light shone through, to look at the wetness on her arms and chest. Only sweat. Drenching, icy sweat.

The dream sickened and abused Anne for days, casting a pall on her daughters' visit. She wanted to say to them, "you can't imagine what a terrible nightmare I had," but she could not. Of course they couldn't imagine it; she could hardly imagine it herself. What would they think of her for dreaming such a thing?

Perhaps the dream had been precipitated by her brother's recent phone call saying that their mother had surgery for cancer again, following ten years of remission. Sonny said he had flown up to be with her; she was fine; it was a small tumor and they got it all. Listening, Anne had wondered at her own detachment--he could have been talking about a stranger--then she realized that at last she had outgrown being needed as the fixer of unpleasant problems, the one called only when things went wrong. She sent her mother an unnecessarily expensive bouquet, relieved that Sonny had gone to be with her.

After the dream, she told her daughters about their grandmother's surgery and they sent cards with friendly notes. Perhaps they would stop by to see her, as they did occasionally, but she would not ask them to go there. Then they packed their cars and drove away, leaving six-year-old Julie for the summer. Anne took Julie along on writing assignments, got her a kitten, then another after an inspirational funeral for the first one, and thought that it must be good for a child to see her family stretching back into the years.

In unguarded moments, the dream still crept into her mind, and Anne began to believe that she ought to visit her mother.

She wanted to take Julie to visit her aunts and uncles and cousins in Pennsylvania. The trip back to Florida would be a hard drive for one day, but the southern college citadel where her mother lived would be a halfway point. Anne thought Julie was a bright child, striking looking with her blue-green eyes, dark hair and great height--as tall as the ten year olds, and she began to believe that her mother would appreciate seeing such an exceptional great-granddaughter.

"We're going on a pilgrimage," she told Julie. Julie regarded her with an amused stare that caught at her heart; once, her children had worn that look.

"What's a pilgrimage?"

"It's a special trip to visit something or someone you love."

"Are we going to see Mommy?"

"Yes, but we'll see your Mommy at the end of the pilgrimage, when I take you home. We're going tol visit Aunt Debbie and Uncle Al and Nicky, then we'll cross the mountains to see Aunt Becky and Uncle Bob and Benjamin and BJ, and who knows what else? On the way up we'll camp out, look at the ocean, see a big city..."

"Can we go to a movie?"

"Sure. And a zoo."

Returning from Pennsylvania, refreshed and dream-free, Anne waited until the last morning to call, reasoning that it would spare her mother the trouble of preparing for a visit. Besides, she slept better not being committed to the visit, having the option of chickening out at the last minute and bypassing Athens altogether from their safe stopover two hours away. She dawdled over breakfast with Julie before calling, resolving a battle of wits over the free child's plate that came with the motel room by eating the child's plate herself, which turned out to be much nicer than the breakfast Julie ordered from the adult menu.

Having won that round, Julie inspected the swimming pool and decided that it was not very inviting, after all, in the damp cloudy morning with waterbugs skating on its surface. There was nothing for it, then, but to phone.

The voice that answered before the second ring sounded strong and very much in charge.

"Mother?"

"What!" The voice was indignant.

"May I speak to Mrs. James?"

"This is Emma James."

"Mother, this is Anne. Sonny told me that you had to go back to surgery last month. I'm in Anderson with Stephanie's little girl, Julie--you've never seen her--we're on our way back to Florida. We'd like to come to see you, if you feel up to a visit."

After a long moment, Emma James said, "Well, come ahead. When will you be here?"

"All we have to do is brush our teeth and load the car. We'll be there in about two hours."

It was almost eleven o'clock when Anne found the cluster of garden townhouses sequestered between the college and the town. In response to a light tap, her mother opened the door immediately.

"This is Mimi," Anne told Julie, and to her mother, "This is Stephanie's little girl, Julie."

Emma James gave them a quick glance and motioned them towards the back of the house. "I'm paying bills, and if I stop I get confused," she explained, leading them to a small sitting room between a formal living room and a patio garden. She left Anne and Julie standing in front of a morning game show blaring forth from a television set, sat down at a desk, and continued the work they had interrupted.

Anne seated Julie and herself in straight-backed chairs and waited, studying the woman at the desk. How long had it been since she had seen her? At least seven or eight years. Emma James' hair was still skillfully ash blond, still thick and full of coarse vitality beneath its perfect coiffure. Her skin seemed unlined--she had often remarked how creaming preserved her skin. Her back was as straight as ever, and the arms under the short-sleeved beige silk blouse were tanned and robust. Not at all frail.

As she thumbed through envelopes and bills, Emma James began to instruct Anne on the importance of managing one's affairs.

"You look marvelous," Anne told her, ignoring the lecture. "How are you feeling? Did you get our flowers?" Emma James laid her pen down quickly.

"Well, I was in intensive care for two weeks, you know. There were so many flowers that, when I could lift my head to see them, I sent them away to the poor people who didn't have any friends. Such a waste, all those expensive flowers. My minister came to see me for an hour every day and just sat with me and held my hand.

"But now," she said, "I'm taking my aerobic dancing class again, and teaching my embroidery classes. I am going to enroll in some classes at the University next semester. Do you know that the University is here?" She began putting bills and checks into envelopes.

"Everyone knows the University is here, Mother. Did I tell you we've been up north to see Debbie and Becky?"

"Yes," she replied. "I suppose Debbie's gotten quite fat."

"No, she's skinnier than I am. She really looks great." Debbie, her oldest, was the only one of her five children her mother had taken any notice of.

"Oh?" Her mother looked disappointed. "Well. She must be working hard, then. Where is she working now, in a convenience store?"

"No, mother." Anne got up and turned the television off.

"She worked in the Comptroller's office the last couple of years, until Al was promoted to President and General Manager, then she had to stop working there because of company policy." Her mother sat silently, with big watchful eyes, the corner of her mouth curled up, and Anne went lamely on, sounding like an apologetic child:

"Becky really looks great, too. She just got a promotion, and Bob has a new job. She's done a wonderful job with their little boys."

"They came to visit me. They got sick because they weren't used to good food."

"I believe Candy and Rob came to see you, too?"

"They were here. She's j-e-a-l-o-u-s."

Not wanting to hear about it, Anne said, "Do you think so? Julie spells quite well." She could feel her face screwing up in a frown, fought to control it. Her mother had always said that she would get wrinkles and her mouth would look like an old hen's behind if she didn't stop frowning. Her mother had always said that everything Anne thought showed on her face.

Ought she try to tell her mother what she'd been doing? She hadn't even told Emma James where she lived now, which made her nightmare visit even more bizarre. Whenever she thought of the nightmare, she wanted to say to her mother, "I had the most terrible dream about you..."

Julie was beginning to wriggle impatiently, so Anne took her hand, saying, "Come, let's look at Mimi's pretty things." When she had gone halfway around the living room, making up stories for the child about the collectibles and crewel embroidery, her mother left her desk and offered to show them through the apartment.

"This is where you will sleep," her mother said, leading them into the guest bedroom. Anne's nightmare returned with sickening clarity, and she protested quickly:

127

"Oh no! We've got to be back in Florida tonight."

"Oh?" she said, looking directly at Anne for the first time. "I was sure you were spending the night. You will have lunch though," she stated, consulting her watch, "it's almost twelve."

"We don't want to put you to any trouble. Perhaps we could take you to lunch?"

"You know restaurant food doesn't agree with me. I've got lunch ready; it's no trouble."

"Then that would be lovely," Anne agreed.

Emma James opened the first closet door in the guest room then, and began to show them new ensembles, describing how she came to buy each and how they coordinated with each other and how much it cost to alter the hem on a jacket ($78) that she'd paid a great price for, and they examined the fabrics and colors of each minutely. Anne complimented her on her good taste--the words echoed back over the decades, rolling over all the times her mother had told her how little taste she had. The times her mother had sent dresses: all two sizes too large, with conspicuous price tags, notes about proper accessories, and dry-clean-only labels at a time when Anne could hardly afford laundry detergent.

While they admired half the closet, Julie looked baffled, unsure whether she should sit on the elegant beds covered with handmade quilts and embroidered and ruffled pillows, or just stand there and wait. Hoping to detour the rest of the closet, Anne asked the child if she would like to use the bathroom, and was rewarded by a tour of both bathrooms and her mother's bedroom.

One corner of Emma James' bedroom was occupied by a large, three-story, colonial doll house set upon a swivel-top table so that it could be turned to provide access to its open back. It was furnished with perfect tiny furniture, accessories, bath fixtures, and a perfect tiny baby.

"This is Steven's," Emma James said proudly. "He's the

only one I have ever allowed to play with it. He spends hours rearranging the furniture--he thinks I don't know how to arrange furniture properly."

A torrent of words poured forth and her eyes flashed and her lips curved happily as she described Steven's feelings about each tiny accoutrement and where she had bought it. Anne wondered who "Steven" was, and they had progressed to the second bedroom of the doll house before she realized that Steven was her seventeen-year-old nephew. His younger brother was not mentioned. Steven must be the current loveable and worthwhile person in her mother's life, which accommodated only one perfect person at a time. There had been a procession of perfect cousins taken everywhere, helped in their careers and held up to Anne as examples for a few years, then discarded with rancor when they crossed her mother.

At least they were on a subject that could include Julie, and the doll house was admired until Anne began to worry about the time and suggested that Julie was probably hungry; could they help with lunch? Julie was always conveniently and enthusiastically, but selectively, hungry. Today the menu included vegetable soup, which Julie didn't like, kiwi fruit, which she'd never seen and therefore wouldn't like, honey dew melon and croissants. Anne didn't know how she felt about croissants.

"Can I set the table?" Julie asked. Emma James agreed, and Anne tried not to appear apprehensive as she carried in the gold-trimmed porcelain plates and bowls, each costing enough to feed Julie and her mother for a week. The mechanics of preparing lunch provided welcome respite from her mother's non-stop talk, which had begun to make Anne's neck ache, and she smiled, nodded, and agreed while she sliced melons and warmed croissants.

"What do you think of Sonny's new home?"

"I haven't seen it," Anne replied. "What's it like?"

"Oh? Why, it's perfectly gorgeous, of course. The pieces I've given them fit it perfectly. You ought to go see it. When he told me he had the opportunity to join Helen's uncle's business right at the time his company changed hands and let him go, I was just delighted to help them get out of *that* area."

"I didn't know you helped them," Anne ventured, fishing. *That* area, she supposed, meant her father's bailiwick.

"Oh, yes, of course. I cashed in some CDs and gave them $100,000 to buy the house."

Well, Anne thought, I won't tell her that my father gave them $20,000 and thought that he was lending them the down payment on the house. Will I tell my father about the $100,000 gift? He would be shocked, and angry at being outdone.

Her mother ate even faster than Anne remembered, talking constantly while her entire lunch disappeared before Anne's soup cooled enough to taste. She was still the consummate consumer, unchanged except to become more of whatever she had been during the years when Anne had cared one way or the other. Julie, who could be a terror at meals, cheerfully ate everything except the kiwis, which she politely tasted. Suddenly depressed because her mother would not appreciate the good manners this six-year-old child was displaying for her benefit, Anne finished the kiwis and the croissants herself and decided to give Julie a double helping of ice cream for dessert.

The conversation soon turned to Anne's father. Emma James' strong, youthful features became more animated, the smokey green eyes shot sparks, venom flowed from lips curved in a scornful half-smile. They were done with Steven and his doll house, the twenty dollars she gave him for breakfast each morning, the umbrellas they selected together at an auction, and the white-water rafting in the mountains before her last surgery. Done with her aerobic dancing and university classes, done with the collectibles from every country in the world except Spain (next year, she said). It was time to review the consuming passion of Emma James' life, her hatred of the man to whom she was married for 17 years-- the passion that probably grew the cancers in her gut, Anne speculated.

Through soup, croissants and fruit, Anne marveled that her mother could remain so bitter for--how long now?--for 40 years after getting what she wanted most in the world: rid of Anne's father. By the time ice cream was served, Anne had become anxious about the effect this sort of talk about her great-grandfather might have on a six-year-old.

"Actually, mother," she inserted into the stream of words, "I don't see how you can remember all the things that have made you so unhappy. I really couldn't sustain that much anger for so long." *Or I wouldn't have come here,* she added silently.

"Do you know what I will never forgive him for?" Emma James cried angrily. "When he came home and told me he had joined the OSS, without asking me, and he went off to Europe and left me to cope with two brats! Two brats!" She spat the last two words out with flecks of saliva, breathing hard.

Anne gave her cowering granddaughter a reassuring hug, remembering that the two brats had been tucked safely away in boarding schools, a reliable live-in maid had tended the fashionable home in Arlington, and her mother only had to cope with being footloose and fancy-free.

"That's not all," Emma James continued, regaining her breath. "I didn't hear from him for six months. For *six* months! I didn't know where he was or how to get in touch with him, and I didn't hear from him!"

"Well," Anne said, pushing her chair back, "I should think that would have been a great relief, mother. We really must get on the road." She began to carry the dishes into the kitchen and Julie scrambled to help.

The table cleared and perfunctory goodbye remarks begun, Anne propelled Julie toward the door. Her mother tugged them back to the sitting room:

"Wait a minute. I want you to see something. There," she said, pulling a newspaper clipping out of a cubbyhole and showing Anne a photograph, "who does that look like?" The white-haired, round-faced woman with large protuberant eyes didn't look like anyone Anne knew, although the eyes reminded her of an aunt. She stared at the photo, trying to guess what she was expected to say.

"It's my cousin, Mavis Barnett," Emma James said, impatiently. "Don't you see the resemblance? She looks exactly like my mother. She's coming to spend a week with me; I haven't seen her for years. I don't see how you can help but recognize her."

"The last time I saw your mother was when I was ten years old. I was very fond of her--she was always good to me. I wish I knew more about her." She did want to know about her grandmother, a woman who was the mainstay of a county filled with cousins and great-uncles and great-aunts and nieces, who kept Anne summers and made dresses for her out of printed flour sacks, and mailed pies to her at summer camp. Anne wanted to understand how that kind woman could have borne her mother, then produced a son who failed at everything and died young, a daughter who took to bars and strangers' beds at sixteen and died young, another son said to be "shocked in the war" who twitched and stumbled and drank his way to an early death, and finally, a beautiful hypochondriac who gave all her expendable parts to surgeons and died a young empty shell.

"Well, you ought to remember her. Your father borrowed the money for our first house from her and never paid her back. Fifteen hundred dollars was a lot of money in those days." Emma James pushed the clipping back in its cubbyhole with an air of swift finality.

"Which way are you going?"

"I'm not sure of the best way to get around Atlanta, but I'm going to Montgomery and then south."

"You need to take 78 to Atlanta. You go down to Broad Street, turn left, and turn left again two blocks up at the light." They had gained the front door. "I'd better lead you there; let me get my car keys. You'll never find it. You'll get lost." She kept insisting.

"No." Anne said. "We're quite good at finding our way around. I have gone all over this country and overseas alone for years and years." Her voice was angry and defensive; she hadn't meant that to happen.

"Well, let me look at you," Emma James said to Julie, as if she were seeing her for the first time, but not touching her, "and see who you look like. You have your mother's skin and height--where did you get those eyes?"

"She was lucky," Anne said. "Good looks, brains, and size. I have a lot of smart, good-looking grandchildren."

"Well, how have *you* been? Are you working?"

"I'm fine, Mother. Of course I'm working. Thanks for lunch--it was a treat."

"Well, it was good to see you. Be careful, now."

"We will." Anne took Julie's hand and pulled her through the doorway into the beckoning sunlight. She took her car keys out of her pocket, and held them while she said the rest of the right things that she thought one ought to say to an aged mother; the keys wrapped securely in her hand radiated warmth and comfort. They waved and smiled as they drove away.

They drove in silence for a long time while Julie gazed out the window. At last, the child asked,

"Are we poor?"

"No, sweetheart, we're rich. We just don't have much money."

"Who was that lady, Grandmommy?"

"She's your mom's grandmother," Anne answered vaguely.

"But you called her mother."

"She is my mother," Anne said, "but it's not like you and your mom and me. We'll talk about it sometime, about a hundred years from now."

Julie giggled. "You're funny, Grandmommy."

"Right, Julie. And I love you."

DON'T GO OUT ALONE

It knows when I am most vulnerable, and when I open the closet door, it leaps out and wraps its arms around my knees, begging,

"Take me out in the sunshine--please--maybe there's a hunt somewhere?"

"You're ridiculous," I tell it, savoring its silky feel and brave colors. "What would people think?"

"Don't you hear the hounds?" The red lining flashes flirtatiously."It's been such a long time. It's so dark in here--you don't know what it is like to live like this."

But I've always known what it's like, and I guess it's time we went out together again. The navy jacket with its black velvet collar and bright red silk lining is like the old friend who gave it to me: elegant, dashing, and a little batty. She gave me the jacket just before she conned us into moving her antique furniture, pregnant mare, and *my* dog for heaven's sake, 1,500 miles to Colorado in our horse van. Later, she traded my German Shepherd to someone in Kentucky, and soon after she turned 39, she phoned collect to tell me she had married and produced a godson for me. I still miss the dog, but I have its teeth marks on the handle of my sewing scissors and where it antiqued an end table.

The jacket is actually a formal riding coat which only looks right with white riding breeches. No matter. In the closet, I find a suitable shirt sent to me by Candy when she quit the banking world for a third child. Grey wool slacks from Stephanie, whose weight fluctuates with her level of manic activity, and navy blue shoes from Debbie, whose arches

135

reject normal footwear, almost match the jacket.

Nothing is quite the right size because they're taller and broader-shouldered, but I don't alter the clothes much because I may "lend" them again. Over the years, other almost-matching pieces arrive to tell me of the changes in the lives of those who have been part of my life. On mornings when only my bra and panty hose originated with me, I go to work feeling like a committee--or a very lucky bag lady.

Except for my jeans, which become most comfortable just before the thin spots wear through, no one except my mother ever exactly said that I was shabby or unfashionable. I do recall a snide remark at a horse trials we held, something about washing my neck, but I think it came from someone who fell at the third cross-country fence. I suspect I am a safe recipient of things too good to throw away because I haven't much interest in clothes (or any taste at all, my mother said), or an easily bruised ego.

The images of me conveyed by the hand-me-downs are often flattering or amusing. There's the ultra smart grey wool suit from another friend who went West in midlife. My waist wasn't that small when I was ten years old, but I suck it in, pleased that she thought I would fit. That friend shed a dour husband of twenty years, got a job on a newspaper on the other side of the Rockies, and packed up the kids and went, managing it all with grace and good humor. Wearing her suit, I remember the great times we shared, and mentally telegraph love across the continent.

After I moved across country, a daughter asked what I'd like for a housewarming present and I said that I needed a socket wrench set or a fireplace poker. Before long, UPS brought a large box from her--a stereo. A barbecue fork, given me by a friend who imagines me entertaining on a patio by a pool, is fine for shifting burning logs while the stereo labors to educate my tin ear.

A few years ago, I bought two cotton sweaters that were just the right colors for a redheaded daughter, an expensive pale pink one that I craved for myself and an inexpensive green one. Guess what came back in my latest care package? "Pink is a good color for you," she wrote; "I've got too much bosom for this." Talk about bread upon the waters.

The blue cashmere cowl neck sweater is much too sexy for me, but it carries nice memories of the beau who gave it to me one Fall. In the Spring, after he drove 140 miles to take me away from the accident at nearby Three Mile Island and I declined to go, he gave me a yellow windbreaker with an alligator on it--and I knew it was over between us. I wear the yellow windbreaker sometimes: it keeps me humble.

I may never wear the Pakistani caftan covered with embroidery and tiny mirrors that glitter and wink at me as if we shared some exotic secret. But if its original owner could picture me in it, who knows? Hand-me-downs pick me up. Does anyone else go out so clad in loving memories?

MOTHER LOVE

The fat man on her porch wore a serious suit and carried a briefcase. Mary thought he looked too grim to be a salesman, and she wasn't expecting any new clients. She opened the screen door a crack and looked at him quizzically.

"Mrs. Whiteacre?"

"Yes."

"James Screed with the Internal Revenue Service." She took the card he thrust at her and put it in her pocket without looking at it. "May I come in?"

"Certainly," she said, opening the door for him. What would he do if she said no? There were many reasons her "cottage industry" could not go on forever, the least of which was the fat man she let into her home.

The career that brought James Screed to Mary Whiteacre's worn wooden porch was only three years old, a venture conceived of despair and disturbing dreams that suggested she was losing her mind along with her farm and everything else. In the dreams, she heard the satisfying plop of long fat dandelion roots freed from soft, moist earth. She realized that pulling weeds had become an obsession when she began to do it covertly, straightening up and pretending she was just walking around or actually going somewhere on her land, whenever neighbors or people passing in cars might see her. Nobody here pulled up weeds. Perversely, they scalped their lawns closer than a shaving commercial, then watered, fertilized, applied weed killers, and scalped them again; but they let their fields go to seed before mowing them, thus effectively scattering weed seeds to the winds that bore them to her pasture.

She couldn't stop pulling weeds because she had to accomplish *something*. Anything. The mindless work distracted her from the reality of being trapped in a place where she didn't fit and shouldn't have come, rejected by employers ("overqualified," she learned, meant too old), alone, and almost broke. She painted the barn and house, pruned the damage from winter storms, advertised her farm and showed it to dozens of disinterested people, hunted for work to pay the mortgage until a buyer came, all to no avail. Writing features for a local arts and entertainment magazine paid as well as the full time jobs available locally, but not enough to survive, and brought unwelcome calls from men who liked her stories, then her voice, and sometimes sounded short of breath while they talked to her on the phone.

One persistent caller had materialized uninvited, unshaven, wearing dress pants slung low under a paunch covered by a greasy army T-shirt, dress shoes with white cotton socks, and carrying a six-pack. Mary sat on the porch with him and drank one beer while he drank five. He crushed each can down to the size of an ashtray and threw it in her yard, staring at her with unblinking eyes while she tried to convince him that she was not for him. She was afraid that he would return. Or that someone worse would come.

When the elbow that had ached from playing tennis in a better life hurt too much from pulling weeds and painting and the regular farm chores, she watched Oprah and despised herself for watching. One day Oprah featured men who blamed their problems on their mothers: impotence, child abuse, wife abuse, adultery, career problems, drugs, alcohol, all because they hated/loved mama and she screwed up their lives.

"Those guys are really serious," Mary thought, astonished. "I could fix that. I know how people with poisonous parents feel, what they need." She wrote an advertisement:

Men: Is your mother still interfering in your life? Escape to a tranquil rural haven and sort out those mother-love/stick-it-to-mama feelings...a weekend of private, caring therapy can turn it around for you.

She mailed the ads and checks, feeling sheepish and embarrassed, and sure nothing would come of it. Nevertheless, she waited, and wondered if there was a law against offering "caring therapy" on the strength of an ancient degree in psychology. She pulled up so many weeds that the pasture looked like a golf course.

After she struck out on the first two responses to her ads, she realized that the callers were hesitant because she was unsure of herself; she hadn't convinced herself that this crazy idea could work. The third caller made an appointment to spend the following weekend with her.

He drove past twice before turning into her lane. Identifying the car as a Volvo on the second pass eased her apprehension, and when he finally shut off the engine and opened the car door, she came down the steps to meet him halfway and offer him her hand.

"Hi," she said, "I'm Mary. Are you nervous?"

"John," he said. "Yeah, I've had a lot of second thoughts about this."

She smiled at him reassuringly. "I'd think there was something really wrong with you if you didn't have second thoughts. But you can leave anytime you feel too uncomfortable, and you are absolutely safe here. That's why I don't want to know your last name and you pay with cash instead of a check; you are not committed and you are anonymous."

"Okay. Now what?" He didn't sound reassured.

"Come in, let me show you around--it's just an old farmhouse, but quiet and private. We'll have a drink and I'll tell you the very little that you need to know about me. The rest of the weekend is yours. We'll work outdoors, simple stuff with our hands, handle horses, talk. Ever been around horses?"

"I'm afraid of horses."

"Good, that's something we can fix, for starts, while we're getting used to each other. You see, horses are afraid of *you*. Don't worry, you won't get hurt and you're going to like it."

Looking skeptical, he got a small bag out of his car and followed her into the house. She liked the look of him. Slender but strong, with distinctive cheekbones, green eyes that looked directly at her, short salt-and-pepper beard and hair. Deep lines in his face, but smooth youthful arms the color of old pine. Light on his feet for his height, walked with toes pointed straight ahead, placing each foot in front of the other. His tightly clenched jaw eased as he looked about the upstairs room that would be his. It was isolated, shaded by the giant pecan tree that sheltered half the house, and filled with the chatter of birds.

"Bathroom's down the hall," Mary told him. "No neighbors except the cows across the road and the horses out back, so you don't have to pull the shade down unless you want to. My room is downstairs, and the walls in this old house are so thick that we can't hear each other. Come on down to the kitchen after you settle in."

At the kitchen table, he declined a beer--"I don't drink," accepted iced tea.

"Are you a teetotaler because of good sense, religion or a problem?"

"Heredity. I don't mind if you have a beer; my friends drink."

"About me," Mary said. "I've been divorced and self-employed for 20 years, raised five kids alone. They're grown, doing fine; one of the things I like best about them is they're all good parents. I was raised by black maids, then spinster schoolteachers in boarding schools; I was 40 years old before I could deal with the fact that my parents didn't have much use for me, didn't even like me. Majored in psychology, been a fair number of places, done more things than most people, and heard more things than I ever dreamed I would. End of subject."

His smile was fleeting, but sincere. That was good, token smiles made her uneasy.

"You been doing this long?"

"Yes." It was true; she had been doing this all her life, involuntarily and without pay. Listening and being there for kids and friends and lovers, until she came to this place, where people she did not care to know lined up to dump on her. She would do what she always had done: listen, accept, reassure.

She learned that John had married at thirty and had sons twelve and thirteen years old. Playing scrabble that night he talked about his wife, a lawyer, "a really good woman and mother;" he was proud of her. They talked about current events and personal affairs interchangeably, with the free exchange possible in a temporary relationship between compatible minds. She let the answering machine take calls and did not play them back until he had gone upstairs to bed.

After the morning chores, they rested on the shaded porch and watched yearling colts playing stallion games, rearing, wrestling in mid air, dropping to their knees, then galloping around the fields in a mad game of tag. He told her that he worked for the Bureau of Indian Affairs; his father was

Indian.

"I knew that when you got out of your car."

"What if I had been black?"

Mary shrugged."That would have been the same as being Indian, your problem, not mine."

Flushing angrily, he got up and went into the kitchen. She heard the beeps of the microwave being set and called to him to bring her some coffee, too. He did not answer, but he returned with two cups, handed her one silently, and sat down beside her.

She put her free hand on his knee. "Please don't misunderstand me. I meant exactly what I said: whether you are an Indian does not concern me."

"You can't possibly know what it is like to be *different*. To be less than other people."

"You're right that I can't know what it is to be another race. But I know a great deal about being different. I also know Indian history; I've researched and written articles on current Indian problems--including your tribe, and I can tell you absolutely that the people who care whether you are Indian or Black, or whatever, are far less than you."

There was doubt in the green eyes, distrust in the twist of his lips. She looked at the dark circles under his eyes and thought that it must be hell to be so vulnerable.

"Okay," he said, finally, and covered her hand on his knee with his.

They played scrabble again that night, and he told her that his parents had married at seventeen because his mother was pregnant. His mother had been the middle daughter of a white merchant in a small Southern city; his father the high school's star quarterback and the son of a hog farmer in Scuffletown, a rural Indian settlement. He had grown up on his grandfather's hog farm in a rambling wooden house packed with dark robust cousins and uncles and aunts, where his mother had faded away interminably, being so pale and delicate for so long that it was hard to remember when she had actually died. He did not know his mother's family.

They watched Saturday Night Live and agreed that it had been funnier in the beginning--everything had been funnier in the beginning, and he said he'd been tortured by impotence from the beginning of his marriage, although he had no problem before he married.

"Does your wife look like your mother?"

"No, she's white but she's a big, tall woman. My mother was small like you."

On the last day, Mary awoke to find coffee made and bitter from sitting on the warmer too long, the horses fed and turned out, and no sign of John. Not in his room or bathroom or the barn. She brewed fresh coffee and sat on the porch. What if she had pushed him too far and he'd done himself some harm? How the hell would she explain that? She finished her second cup of coffee before she saw him come out of the far side of the woods, walking with his shoulders slumped and his eyes on the ground.

When he reached the porch, she said, "You forgot to tuck your pants in your socks. Better take your shoes off, roll up your pants and check for ticks. How about some fresh coffee?"

He nodded and began to untie his shoes. She brought coffee, checked the back of his shirt for ticks, and sat down beside him. His eyes were sunken, his face drawn.

"Are you all right?" she asked.

"Yes. Really. I just didn't sleep, couldn't stop thinking."

"I'm sorry. I hope it's not my fault."

"It is. I kept remembering things I had completely forgotten. Things my mother told me when I was a little kid."

He drank his coffee. Mary waited. Words came in an angry, embarrassed rush:

"She was always sick, in bed most of the time. She told me my father hurt her because his penis was so big, he made her sick. She died when I was fifteen."

She fought to suppress a smile. "Go on, you're an intelligent man, you know your father's penis didn't kill your mother. Most women like big penises."

"You don't know."

"Do you know how many times you have said 'you don't know' to me? Maybe I do know. If you're worried about the size of your penis, better let me have a look at it," she teased him.

"Is that supposed to be part of your therapy?" His face was a tortured mixture of fear and longing.

"It certainly was not planned, but it seems logical to go on since we've made this much progress. Since you were up all night thinking about this."

"All right."

"Not here," she said, and took his hand, like ice inside her warm one, and led him inside to her bedroom, a chaste, shadowy room where chimney swifts twittered in the chimney of an old brick fireplace. Light filtered in from the adjoining bathroom's small window, which framed hollyhocks in the dooryard and through the wood-slatted blind covering the bedroom's only window, reflecting softly on a satin bedspread.

He pulled his hand away from hers. "I can't take my clothes off in front of you."

"It's only a body." She thought she sounded remarkably detached. "I've probably seen better and worse. I'll take mine off first; my old bod will make you laugh so hard you won't care."

He smiled, and unfastened his belt. She smiled back, and pulled her sweatshirt over her head.

"You don't look like a grandmother," he said, accusingly.

"This is not about me," she said, unbuttoning his shirt. She slipped it off his shoulders. "You are a very attractive man. I'll bet your father was, too."

"He was. My mother thought she married beneath her, and he was ashamed of that, but he was a good man."

"And so are you." She untied her tennis shoes, stepped out of them and dropped her jeans to the floor, seeing out of the corner of her eye that he was duplicating her actions.

"This isn't so hard, is it?" She looked down, and laughed: the front of his boxer shorts jutted out like a tent. "Sorry, bad choice of words." He laughed, too; she hugged him for the laughter and they clung together for a moment.

"Back to business," she said, stepping back, and he pulled his shorts down.

"That's nice," she said. Her tone was serious, but she could not stop smiling. "Better than average, hardly threatening."

But when Mary touched it, it grew wonderfully, and she held it against her and it came alive. It took a while to get it all inside her--God, maybe his mother had been right--or maybe she had rusted shut from disuse--but she could not risk the fragile moment by hunting a lubricant. She almost laughed again, remembering that the only lubricant was out in the barn for examining mares, and on that thought, he entered her fully and began to work powerfully, steadily, breathing like a marathon runner at the end of the race. She wanted him to keep fucking her for the rest of her life. He was direct, tender, urgent, and totally unsophisticated.

He stayed inside her after he climaxed, with his arms around her and his face nestled on her shoulder. He dozed, and she stroked his thigh and back tenderly, admired his rosy, youthful skin, studied the tired lines in his middle-aged face and caressed his surprisingly soft beard, and thought fondly that he was just what she needed, a lean mean fucking machine. She wondered if he was really asleep because he still moved inside her, and she squeezed back, and worried about how he was going to feel about this later. When he tilted his head back to look at her, she asked, again,

"Are you all right?"

"Oh God, yes. Never better."

When he went upstairs to shower, Mary stood before the mirror looking at herself in wry amusement. She certainly didn't look the part she had just played. A face often mistaken for someone else, the face of a listener, now wearing a new healthy glow and a softening of tense lines. Baby-fine short dark hair streaked with grey and sunburned glints of red and yellow, curling when the weather was right, limp when it wasn't. Sturdy shoulders, not much bosom but still in its original neighborhood. A waist born middle-aged. Nice fanny, good legs and slender ankles spoiled by big ugly feet. Big, worn hands--not like John's mother, whose hands had been small, soft and pale. She was definitely another kind of mother. She dressed slowly, then pulled the neck of her sweatshirt up over her nose and inhaled the warm musky smell of sex.

Long after John had gone back to wherever he came from, she often thought that she couldn't have asked for a better start in her new career.

Between clients she cleared her mind of the last one's problems, planned menus of the next one's favorite foods, and put the manure from the stalls in a big pile for them to spread on the pastures. Most men loved doing the routine chores that kept the farm going; they laughed when she assured them that toting five-gallon buckets of water and shoveling manure would build up their pectorals, and worked harder.

They sat on the porch and counted bird calls; a former eagle scout identified 32 birds. They walked together in the woods and city men learned to recognize poisonous plants and snakes, local trees and shrubs; in cold weather they followed deer trails and collected firewood. They held mares to be bred by her stallion and stayed up at night to help deliver new foals, entranced by the natural affection between stallion and mare, the bonding between mare and foal. The horses became immaculately groomed and totally spoiled.

Those in residence when colts were gelded were stricken to the core by the beautiful young animal lying helpless while "his manhood"--they cried--was neatly sliced out and the spermatic cord crushed. She pointed out that the procedure was quite kind, tidy, and pain-free compared to the macho throwing and cutting of unanesthetized animals practiced in "the good old days." When they mourned the colt's "loss of a sex life," she explained that only the strongest and quickest males reproduced in the wild; only in civilization did all males assume the right to screw and make babies. Besides, wasn't it better to live the life of a beloved, pampered gelding than to be mishandled by men and kicked by mares, or assaulted by other stallions, in an endless struggle to produce offspring of little commercial value?

Evenings, tired and well fed, they watched television, listened to records, or played card games or scrabble. She cared for them unquestioningly, and if they wanted to do things for her, she accepted and thanked them. Mostly, she listened and accepted; in sharing her thoughts about the farm, the woods, the animals, she was saying all the things she had wanted to say to men all her life, and she was being paid for it.

It was rather like running a camp for large disturbed boys, all so engrossed in themselves that none guessed that deep inside her, like a bone spur, lived a small sharp fear of letting these unhappy, vulnerable strangers into her home.

Some men made love to her, some did not; it was not a thing to be contrived. What worked was what they said to her, at first faltering, then fulminating until they couldn't seem to stop talking. They talked about themselves, their mothers, fathers, lovers, friends and enemies; about work, sex and death. They bragged, lied, and ultimately told as much truth as they needed to tell. She felt an odd affection and empathy for each, and rarely ever thought of any of them again.

When the men arrived, they always found her gate standing open. When they went away, she was intrigued to see that they always closed the gate carefully behind them and latched it.

"Is there a problem with my return?" Mary asked James Screed.

"We have some questions," he said. She led him into the living room, motioned him to the sofa. He looked around the room for a long time before he plunked his briefcase on the coffee table, opened it and took out a file. Mary sat on the sofa next to him, close enough to read her name on the file.

"Your income for last year was $32,500," he stated. Mary nodded. "Bank records reveal that $25,800 was deposited in cash, in varying amounts, usually on Monday mornings."

"I paid taxes and social security. What is the problem?"

"The problem is the cash. When we see large cash deposits from unknown sources, we suspect money laundering."

"Money laundering! That's nonsense! None of the deposits was that large and I submitted a Schedule C. Do you want to see a copy?"

"I have a copy of your return right here."

Mary studied him as he rummaged through the file: late thirties, sandy thinning hair, plump baby cheeks and a pursed little mouth. Pale cold eyes. Short white fingers like uncooked sausages. He had gained weight since he bought that off-the-rack suit. She shivered, suddenly chilled; this man was one too many intrusive strangers in her life. She wondered if her single-parent daughter, stressed by corporate demands and a pre-adolescent child, might welcome a reliable live-in grandmother.

Screed's lips moved as he read the Schedule C line by line, then he held it up and waved it at her triumphantly.

"This shows $6,700 income from writing and stud fees deposited in checks. Do you have records verifying the source of that income?"

"Yes."

"I will need to examine those records, and the records verifying the source of the $25,800 income from..." he peered at the form, "counseling, it says here."

"Am I being audited? I thought you usually mailed a notice to come in and bring records."

"We are handling your case in-home to better investigate the reason behind these irregularities."

"What irregularities?"

Screed looked down his nose at her as if she were quite dense. "The cash, Mrs. Whiteacre, the source of the cash, and the reason for receiving cash from this source."

"It is quite simple," she told him. "I am paid in cash because of the absolute confidentiality of my counseling service. To protect my clients and help them feel at ease, I do not accept checks and I use only their first names on the deposit slips."

"But you have records of their last names?"

"No," she admitted, "I don't. Never wrote any last names down, don't remember any."

"Do you have phone numbers? How did you get in touch with them?"

"I never called them, they called me. If I had to return a call, I destroyed the number later. I promised that they would be protected, and they were. They are."

James Screed closed his briefcase and snapped the locks with a flourish, smiling like a man sucking a lemon. "This looks like a clear cut case of laundering, probably drug money."

"So send in the DEA," Mary said calmly.

"Or a case of soliciting," he said ominously. "How would your children feel about a prostitution charge?"

"Soliciting! My clients and I talked about their mothers!"

Screed's plump cheeks quivered indignantly. "That will be the worst part of it, if you are prosecuted on a morals charge, using a sacred name like "mother" to advertise your so-called service. It's un-American! We have seen your ads: I can imagine what a jury would think of "stick-it-to-mama" therapy."

"*A sacred name like mother*," Mary repeated thoughtfully. "You must have loved your mother very much."

The pale eyes turned pink and watery. "My mother was a saint," he said, thrusting his chin forward and giving his trousers a hitch as if he felt them slipping down.

"Tell me about her," Mary said softly, putting her hand gently on his shoulder, and he began.

He withdrew with a satisfying plop, reminiscent of the sound of dandelion roots giving up the soft moist earth. His face was unpleasantly wet against her breast, and her back ached where he had thrust a sofa cushion under her. He shuddered, raised his scarlet face, and looked at her in horror.

"You tricked me."

"What an odd thing to say. It was not my idea; I thought it was what *you* wanted."

"You won't get away with this; there are laws."

"IRS agent rapes and blackmails grandmother," she said thoughtfully. "Agent cries out "mother!" at climax. Nice headlines." She disentangled her legs, smoothed her dress down, crossed the room briskly and picked up the phone.

"No one would believe you."

"DNA typing," Mary said. "Do I *look* like a seductress?"

She dialed; he dove across the room and squashed the connection before the first ring.

"Truce," Screed said. His face had gone white and glistening with sweat. Trousers around his ankles, he clutched the phone with one plump hand and covered his genitals with the other.

"Truce," Mary said. "Look, I've been wanting to get out of this business and move, anyway. I will, now. Can you handle this inquiry so the IRS will leave me alone?"

He nodded.

"I am going to report an assault," she told him cheerfully, "have the tests to identify an unknown assailant, and have the crime lab check for hair and fiber samples. But I won't give them your name unless the IRS bothers me again. It's just insurance, Mr. Screed."

When he had fastened his trousers, smoothed his suit coat and picked up his briefcase, Mary put her hand out. He took it with obvious distaste, still looking white and ill.

"It was nice to meet you, Mr. Screed," she told him, feeling quite kindly towards him. "You really ought to get some therapy to help you sort out your feelings about your mother."

POSTSCRIPT FROM THE GOLDEN YEARS

He leans against the fence and stares reproachfully at me.
His lower lip hangs open pathetically at one corner, probably
a result of surgery the year he got overconfident and his
favorite visiting mare broke his jaw. I know this act well. He
will stand there with his ears pricked forward and that
reproachful look on his face as long as I'm in sight, like a
frail, wasted little old man on a nursing home porch hoping
that someone will push his wheelchair out into the sunshine.

There is a sadness in old stallions. This old horse will run no
more races, he creeps about the farm, favoring his stiff old
joints. Spring brings only a few mares to breed, only a few
foals that might set new records. He was so vital and
ambitious when we both were young and foolhardy; now he
is weary and cautious. I feel his sadness. I had pictured us
growing old together; now I am glad that I will outlive him,
won't have to worry that he is left behind cold or hungry or in
pain.

Okay, horse, I tell him, *you win.* Seeing me tote the tack
and grooming kit out, Bayaref heads towards his stall in a
slow, deliberate, Godfather walk. He detours to the two-year-
olds, flattens his ears tight against his head and points his
nose at one, then the other: *You, and you, OUT.* Each colt
makes an obeisance, cringing back onto its hind legs, and
scurries away. There is a gleam in Bayaref's eye and his
drooping lip is tucked up into a smirk.

We have always had an understanding: on the ground, I'm in

153

charge. When I'm on the ground, people say they can't believe this horse is a stallion, but he and I know that's no big deal. He stands like a statue while I scrape away the mud. Bayaref could find mud in the Sahara. It's hard to tell that he has turned white with age because he is black and brown and yellow from the different soils in the pasture. The rubber curry makes coarse tracks in the dried mud, then the brush makes fine tracks and the dust swirls up my nose and into my eyes. The only way to ride a clean Bayaref is to wash him and cross-tie him until he dries. As I brush and cough and wheeze, he yawns, confident that he will regain my sympathy when I brush the "honorable hunting scars," the bowed tendons, broken elbow, splints, and irretrievable bone chips that he has earned "hunting" a win, a mare, or a way into a different pasture or stall.

I gently brush mud out of the deep hollows over his still-bright eyes, and put on two saddle pads to compensate for the swayed back of old age. He seems narrower lately, though he was never a wide horse--"both front legs come out of one hole" as aficionados of beefy horses say. *Poor old man.* Head hanging, he follows me out like a horse going to the knackers, and waits quietly while I fasten the gate behind us.

A toe in the stirrup, a swing up, I am in the air above the saddle--and he is halfway down the lane, ears pricked happily. *Just wait, little buddy.* I stop him, check my stirrups and tighten the girth, and we're off at a pleasant, ambling walk on the buckle. Once he had a great variety of walks, trots and canters, and a hand gallop and a win-or-die gallop. Now he only offers me choices between the going-to-the-knackers walk, purposeful working trots or extended trots that hardly touch the ground, and a working canter. Maybe old stallions forget things, like old men. I don't want to know whether he remembers the win-or-die gallop.

I have a long memory of Bayaref's old ambitions, so most

days we work familiar roads where he's quiet and bored. Today we will do a ten-mile round trip, taking a new road to the crossroads and then heading west on the narrow grass verge along the highway. Under saddle, he feels sure-footed and enthusiastic, and I think how much fun it might be to do a little 25-mile endurance ride.

We come upon a place he hasn't seen before, a barren, surrealistic hillside populated with stumps, goats, a pony stallion, and donkeys. The goats and donkeys are the same color and about as lively as the stumps, but in an adjoining woods pigs and piglets lurk in the shadows and fight and squeal. Simultaneously, a donkey-stump moves and a pig savages another with a wild shriek, and Bay bolts a quarter-mile down the road before I realize I am still on him and doing fine. We cross the highway and trot briskly towards the crossroads. I walk him through the crossroads on a loose rein; *take it easy, little buddy,* I say, and he flicks an ear back at me politely.

Heading west now, in a good workout. The sun and wind are perfect. This is not an extended trot, it's a flying trot. We're hydroplaning--I can barely hear his hoofbeats. Beer cans sail out of the grass and clatter onto the pavement--this horse could have been a great soccer player. He looks down the long straight highway like he wants to eat it up, ears intently forward, not moving his head at all to the trot. There is soft, steady contact between my hands and his mouth, no pulling or foolishness, and I let him canter the last half mile to a railroad crossing.

I walk him to a grassy patch near the railroad, and look at my watch. We have done four miles in fifteen minutes. He's dry and his respiration and pulse are normal; we could do 16 miles easily in an hour. I'll let him pick a little grass, then we'll do another mile and go home. *You're a good little buddy, Bayaref,* I tell him.

Bayaref snatches a couple of mouthfuls of grass and heads down the highway again, fast. *Whoa! What's this, little buddy?*

Let go, fool, he says, making circles with his nose and doing half-passes down the road, *let me go, they're getting ahead of us!* This horse acts like a bee stung him.

Exuding patience and firmness, I walk Bayaref back to the grassy patch, only it's more piaff than walk, pat him and reassure him. Fighting to turn and fly to some imaginary finish line, he dances dangerously close to the pavement where cars race to church. Heading home is always a real downer for Bay, so I turn him back the way we came and push him forward on a loose rein, sitting deep in the saddle and holding him with my legs. He does a couple of irritated crow-hops, whirls around and collects himself for a mad dash west, ending my pretense of loose-reined control.

Maybe he doesn't know this is the way home. Do I want to do four miles of half-passes and piaff? *Whoa, you pig!* This horse acts like he's got a lighted stick of dynamite up his rump.

I dismount and walk Bayaref down the highway towards home. Actually he is walking me down the highway. After a quarter mile he stops pulling. I mount again and we do more half-passes and piaffs. *Old fool should have done these when we wanted a dressage horse.* I dismount so Bayaref can walk me down the highway again.

A car pulls up beside us, and a middle-aged man asks, "You all right?"

"Fine, thanks. He came up a little sore," I lie, trying to look nonchalant.

"Looks all right now."

"Yeah. He's just sore carrying weight. Thanks."

"Fine lookin' horse." He takes off with a screech of rubber.

The sun is cooking me. I'm sweating like a horse and Bayaref is cool and dry. Are people watching and snickering behind their window shades at the crossroads? I climb back into the saddle, and he does pirouettes like he used to do waiting for the starter's flag. I get off and walk him another half mile. Am I going to walk a 24-year old horse all the way home because he has delusions that this is a race, because he scares me when he dances around like a crazed ballerina?

There isn't room for us to walk side by side on the verge, so I walk on the highway, where the hot road burns painfully through my thin sneakers. Bayaref's races were in the fall, when I stood in cool sand or mud to watch and felt only the pain of fear for his safety. I still see him run as clearly as when I stood by the rail with my heart twisted in a knot. He always ran the same race: breaking first and leading to the first turn; taking up then, letting the other horses come up around him until the final turn; then a fierce last furlong drive to finish first--which he'd done nine times out of twelve and been in the money the other three. Then he would fight us to try to get back to the track and run in the next race.

But that was eons ago. Why can't I have a pleasant hack now, instead of being pulled, stumbling, down the highway?

We've been together since he was a leggy two-year-old that looked like a yearling; now he's 96 in human years, depending upon whom you believe. He's stayed longer than my kids! Bred in the California hills near his sire, he was shipped to me in Florida, I took him to Pennsylvania, lent him to a friend in Colorado for two years, took him to North Carolina, to Texas, to Indiana: an aging Queen of the Gypsies and her faithful steed on their way to the knackers. He hasn't changed his attitude in a quarter of a century--he has just adapted his behavior to accommodate old age.

Like dressage: He still loves to demonstrate movements precisely, accurately, but whenever he does a whole test, he memorizes it. Then along about the second or third movement, you can feel the recall click in his mind--*I know this, and I'll do it MY WAY*. Like four-foot fences that keep him from where he'd rather be: until late middle age he hopped over them, then he scrambled over them, now he pops off the top boards to make an appropriate size jump for an old horse. Boards too tight? He entices the horse on the other side to crash through. I can't figure how he does some things, like escaping the stall I put him in when the creek rises. Next morning, the stall is empty, and I ask my daughter and granddaughter, "Did you let Bay out? No? Come look at this..." We agree there are no marks from jumping an undisturbed four-foot door--as if he still could! No evidence of wriggling through a high narrow window. But Bayaref is in the pasture, unmarked and unruffled, lower lip tucked up into a smirk.

But he still does good things for me, too. He leads yearlings onto their first trailer or van, comforts them when they're frightened, moves a balky horse for me with a threatening shake of his head or a nip on its fanny. He still tries to help me do whatever needs doing; and with infinite patience he still finds ways to do what *he* wants to do.

The donkeys and stumps and goats come in sight and I can feel Bayaref let down, decide that the race is over, and his breathing slows. For the fourth time, I climb back into the saddle. I am in charge again.

We do a brisk trot, then that flying extended trot, and a smooth canter. We bound up the steep banks by my lane and arrive with a grand flourish--he is so sure this is the finish line that I can almost hear the crowd. The mares look up from the pasture disdainfully, and go back to stuffing themselves.

Bayaref is enormously pleased with himself, but for the wrong reasons, and he still owes me a couple of miles. He shuffles a mile in the other, boring, direction with his nose practically on the ground like a bird dog. Returning home, I let him enjoy an exuberant trot, then a canter, and when a car passes us Bay shows off like he always does when he thinks someone is watching, arching his neck and extending his stride. *Good little old buddy,* I tell him, hugging his neck before I slide off. Pulse 30, respiration 8. Hmmmm.

Hosing the sweat off Bayaref, I think about that 25-mile endurance ride again, just a little ride but a long way for an old guy like Bayaref. If we could ride along with a slow, uncompetitive horse, we could probably do it, Bayaref and me. I picture us following a large sleepy mare, too wide to pass on the trail and too high to jump over, for 22 miles. Make that two large sleepy mares, both in season. Then we'll swing around the mares, and I'll let him gallop to the finish like the winner he will always be. I can almost hear the crowd.

I lead Bayaref through the gate and take his bridle off. He follows me back to the fence, leans on it, and stares reproachfully at me while I hang the saddle pad on the line and hose the sweat-extruded mud out of it. He doesn't move when I pick up the saddle and bridle and take them inside. When I return for the grooming kit, he is still there, a frail, wasted little old man waiting for some sucker to push his wheelchair out into the sunshine.

SUNDAY DINNER

"Let's take a vacation," he said. "Go somewhere and relax for a few days. You could get away, couldn't you?"

A warning bell tinkled faintly in her head. "What kind of vacation do you have in mind? What would we do?"

"A nice resort where we could sit by the pool and unwind. Good food, no pressures. Maybe Vegas--we could see some shows, gamble a little, and sleep late; really get to know each other." His smile was beguiling, boyish.

"I don't think vacations are a good way to get to know people," she said, and gave the rice a couple of distracted stirs before she remembered that stirring would make it gummy. "I think you get to know people by living and working with them."

"Shall I put the coffee on? How's your new coffee maker working? I told my kids about your balancing act with the parts from those two old coffee makers," he said. "They died laughing."

"Yes, please make some coffee," she said, missing the old jury-rigged coffee pot hidden away in the cupboard for his weekend visit. The new automatic coffee maker that he had bought for her began to burp impersonally. In retaliation for the stir, the rice turned gelatinous; perhaps she should start a new pot of rice before cooking the steaks. She put a lid on the problem and tried to concentrate on her lover's friendly patter.

"I went by mamma's this morning to take her some paper towels--did I tell you about finding ten cartons of paper towels in the attic?"

160

"Yes, you told me."

"We had no idea my wife bought cases of everything that came on sale at the PX; she bought like she knew she was going to die. Anyway, mamma had taken her car out without letting any of us know. I told you how she drives." Chuckling, he imitated his mother's erratic steering.

"I called all my daughters and no one knew where she might have gone, so I just had to wait for her and hope she remembered how to get back home. I was just about to call the police to report her missing and call you to say I'd be late, when she came weaving up the driveway."

"Maybe your mother's more competent than you suspect. I really think she manages very well."

"I am serious about getting away together, you know," he said. "I talked to my kids about it and they thought it was a great idea."

"Having an affair with the children's blessings seems odd, doesn't it? Do all your children approve?" *Stop it*, she told herself; *stop challenging everything he says.*

He smiled tolerantly. "Lily keeps asking when you are going to spend the night again. She really enjoys talking to you--I can't stay up late enough to talk to her, with that crazy schedule she keeps. She'll never marry, you know, but I suppose she will be able to live alone one day."

"I wouldn't mind if she lived with us--if we did marry. She's a wonderful girl, the way she accepts her handicap. But I think your other children feel it's too soon for you to have a serious relationship."

"I ought to call Lily after dinner; she had trouble with her car again. And I ate her half of the banana again this morning," he chuckled; "she'll have something to say about that. Now, what about that vacation?"

She turned the heat off under the rice, put the steaks under the broiler and set the timer.

"It might be fun to go sailing or white-water rafting, or even canoeing," she offered.

"I don't think my shoulder would hold up," he said, grimacing and clutching his shoulder in anticipated pain. "You'd spend the whole time taking care of me. Besides, I get enough exercise taking care of my yard."

"Oh. I was thinking of fresh air and fun, really. Perhaps we could go somewhere very different, like Nova Scotia or Alaska, and just wander around, seeing how other people live."

"Too cold," he said, refilling their glasses with ice and scotch, "too rugged. I just want to relax with you."

"How about the Bahamas? Some of the out-islands are quite lovely and restful, but different. Interesting native food, bed and breakfast inns, boat trips between islands."

"And mosquitos and tropical sun. You know what the sun does to my skin."

She didn't know, but she could imagine the effect of tropical sun on his white skin, which was remarkably free of the freckles that plagued most redheads.

"How about the Caribbean?" she asked. "Mexico? Or a short cruise--we could do the Mississippi River. We might meet some interesting people."

"Fine, as long as the natives speak English, but I'm not interested in Montezuma's revenge or rubbing elbows with third world crowds. I see enough people at work. We ought to just enjoy each other; I'll tell you more about my family and you can tell me all about yours."

The tocsin in her head became a four-alarm alert, drowning out the buzz of the kitchen timer. She turned away from him and began tearing lettuce into bite-sized pieces.

"Well, when can you get away?"

"It would be very difficult for me to find someone to look after the horses and my house."

"Oh, you could get a friend to stop by and feed them. Just lock everything up and leave the lights on."

"That's a lot of responsibility to leave to someone else," she protested. "Besides, I can get into this house in five minutes without a key. And there is another problem: I can't afford a vacation and I wouldn't feel right about letting you pay for it."

"Hey, I wouldn't dream of letting you spend a cent. It's my treat; I want us to *really* get to know each other."

That was true, he could afford it. After retiring as a Lieutenant Commander with a comfortable pension, one of the "good old boys" had asked him if he knew anything about estimating construction costs. "Nope, not a thing," he'd said, and they gave him the job anyway, paying him twice what she was able to earn--and she knew how to estimate construction costs. She thought, not for the first time, that she would kill for a job like that, but she would not settle for enjoying its benefits vicariously.

He persisted: "Why don't you get one of your kids to look after things so you can get away?"

"They'd come if I needed help, but I couldn't ask them to leave their jobs and families to come down here so I can go off to have a good time with someone they don't even know."

He took her shoulders and turned her away from the salad bowl, looking wise, paternal, and scornful.

"They'd be happy for you to have a good time. I don't see why you make everything so hard. Besides, you raised them; they owe you."

She turned back to the salad and thought about that. He was always so sure how things were supposed to be. When his wife of 28 years had been under a respirator for two weeks, he was sure it was time to let her go; remembering that gave her a sudden chill. She poured too much dressing on the salad, making it soggy, and took the steaks from under the broiler. Her steak had become grey and dry, the way he liked it, while his was still enticingly rare. Would it be rotten to give him the smaller steak so she could have the rare one? On the other hand, it was her steak, and her scotch that he was drinking. .

"Actually," she began, "I've been on four vacations in my whole adult life and none as a child." She took his hands and clasped them inside hers, smiling fondly at him, relishing the smooth feel of his hands, so unblemished, so skillful at giving pleasure.

"I'm glad I went on the two vacations I took with the kids. The other two were for me, and I thought they would lead to wonderful things, but they led to sad and rather profound changes in my life.

"Besides," she continued, "I'm not good at relaxing or at small talk. I make inane remarks, I get antsy, and my neck begins to hurt from sitting in one position." She hesitated, studied his face for clues, and plunged on: I relax by doing something physical like sports, or playing bridge or scrabble, or working on something that totally occupies my mind. I don't know how to explain it to you; I just don't fit the kind of vacation that you describe."

Disappointment flickered in his bland blue eyes, but before she could put her arms around him in comforting apology, his expression congealed and hardened, like the rice and the steak. He didn't believe her.

"I'm sorry," she said.

"Well, think about it." The warmth and enthusiasm were gone from his voice. "See what you can do."

"Okay," she said. "I'll try." She gave him the bigger steak, and the rice off the top where it wasn't so gummy.

TRANSITIONS

After seven fecund springs, my Thoroughbred mare has taken a well-deserved rest. Relieved that she did not settle after slipping a three-months fetus last fall, I hold her while my ancient stallion mounts her. This is the first year he has needed assistance in breeding a mare. This will be my first spring without a new foal in a quarter of a century.

Around me, other rites of spring continued unassisted. Next door, my neighbor's cats have filled every nook and cranny with kittens. The lake in my pasture is swarming: five pairs of Canadian geese lead flotillas of two, five, five, six and two goslings, and in the wake of a lone, plain brown duck I've never seen before, seven tiny balls of down bob on choppy waters. There is a line from a song: "My heart knows where the wild goose goes..." The wild geese are here, where they have become welfare waterfowl.

Adrift among the waterfowl families, there is a lone Canadian goose, hawked and hounded ferociously from family to family by both goose and gander.

A lone blue heron has returned, too, but the geese pay him no mind. The former owners said the heron and his mate had been around for years and years, until he returned alone last spring. I've heard they mate for life, and now he--or she--continues a solitary life in the old pattern. Apparently there are no retirement villages or younger mates for old heron widowers or widows.

Like the waterfowl, horses develop deep, lasting

165

attachments, but the bonding is for friendship, not as mates. None of my stallions ever developed the friendships that mares and geldings often do. My last old stallion has been affectionate towards all his mates, at least as long as they were in season, although some he loved obsessively and others he only tolerated kindly. Like some small men, he was really turned on by big tall females, even though sometimes we had to stand them in a ditch so he could mount them.

The widowed blue heron and the lone Canadian goose seem symbolic because for some years, in the back of my mind, I have contemplated the ultimate solitude of my old stallion. He is 28 years old, 112 in human years, and he has been my friend and ally, comfort and nemesis, for 26 years. He stayed longer than the children did.

Acknowledging the end of my old friend's life was not a sudden decision, but a realization that grew as slowly as the infirmities of age. Ten, fifteen years ago, there were only new tribulations to be survived:

Racing on a slick muddy track, he bowed both front tendons, finished second, and fought us to return to the track and run in the next race (the bugle call to the post always drove him mad with desire, as did the baying of the hounds). The tendons healed in 30 days, but he sounded marginally off when trotting downhill on a paved road, and x-rays showed a small bone chip, floating free between the cannon bone and sesamoid. Since it was not our practice to trot downhill on pavement, he returned to racing where he did better than ever.

In his fourteenth spring, his favorite seventeen-hand visiting Thoroughbred mare broke his jaw, requiring surgery and several weeks of nursing care. When he was 17 years old, another mare broke his elbow, and another vet said he was too old for surgery. The elbow healed, with no apparent consequences.

These tribulations and many lesser ones passed, and early

signs of impending age crept in. Black clumps of melanoma, that plague of grey horses, appeared, grew, threatened, subsided. Some went away, new ones came. In his 22nd year he grew two sarcoid tumors, one just behind his elbow and one on his flank, then melanomas grew in the middle of the sarcoids, and I assumed this oddity was the beginning of the end. The sarcoid and melanoma combinations went away without treatment. I couldn't guess how many melanomas might be growing internally, and after the first decade, one tends to forget to check external melanomas regularly.

He must have been 20 or 21 years old when I realized that he had become swaybacked and his saddle no longer fit him properly. Deep hollows developed above his eyes, and grain fell out of his mouth as he slowly chewed his meals. Floating his worn old teeth didn't help, but switching to pelleted feed did.

The horse that should have been named Lightning began to move like a glacier, and now rarely ran for the sheer joy of it. He found less strenuous methods of accomplishing whatever he wanted to do. He quit jumping four-foot fences, and learned to stick his head under the top rail and pop it off so he could hop over a two-and-a-half foot fence. Obstacles that he once jumped or climbed over, he now wiggled under, moved aside, dismantled or unfastened and took down. We never figured out he managed some escapes, or how he did it all with so little fuss and never hurt himself.

At age 26, if the other horses left him out in the pasture after dark, he could no longer see well enough at night to find his way to the barn, and he would wait, patiently, until I came to walk him in. We walked in very slowly and quietly, a major change in our lives together.

He endured these infirmities patiently and accepted my aid with dignity. When each new infirmity appeared, I knew that it would not go away . . . but he compensated so well that it was easy for me, too, to accept it as he did.

In the spring and early summer of his 27th year, I saddled him and went for long walks, where he checked out the scenery, occasionally broke into a brief trot, paused to be admired by anyone who might be along the road and, for the first time in his life, he never pretended there was a race to be made out there. One day we stayed out longer than usual, and as he approached our lane he walked slower and slower. He stopped dead at the beginning of our long lane, sighed, turned his head, and gave me a long, sad look. I got off and walked in beside him.

In the middle of that summer, my mare had a partial intestinal impaction and she and the foal went to the veterinarians for three days. The old stallion was depressed, hardly touching his grain and moping about the barn instead of grazing in the pasture. He greeted her return with wild enthusiasm; she greeted him with a kick that fractured his jaw again, low on the mandible at the beginning of the molar teeth.

He could chew, very slowly and with much slobbering, and he subsisted on mashes for several weeks while the jaw abscessed minute fragments of bone through the gaping, draining wounds that developed. Aesthetically, he was revolting, but his spirits were unquenched. In four months, all but one small abscess had healed, and the only sequelae of his injury was difficulty in chewing hay. Mornings, I found chewed and spat out clumps of hay in his stall.

It was like taking care of an aged parent or a terminally ill friend, except that there are no social resources. No support group, no living will. My sole decision when to pull the plug, an objective decision fragmented by subjective ties: Identifying with his aging. Our shared history. His history of prevailing over all catastrophes (which I tend to mistake for a Lazarus syndrome). My loss of his unjudgemental love. I always said that when the pain outweighs the pleasure in life, it is time to let go, but have I waited too long, considered my loss, not his?

The icy winds and record subzero temperatures of winter took a cruel grip on my old stallion. When intractable pain came, it was hard for me to accept, although I should have judged its extent sooner. He had always been ambitious and competitive to the core, never giving in to injury. The mornings when he walked out of his stall haltingly, with great difficulty, I said "This is it, it's all over." Then he would warm out of his stiffness and soreness, and I would postpone the inevitable. I thought his good hours outnumbered the bad.

Spring would bring relief. Overnight, spring brought a pain in his left front foot so excruciating that he nearly fell when he tried to put weight on it. Classic symptoms of a developing abscess, I thought, and the blacksmith and veterinarian thought so, too. Trimming, poultices and time failed to work; butazolidin brought little relief.

Mornings, I found pinkish stains on his groin and inner thighs, and swollen lymph nodes. I could guess where the melanoma has traveled.

The heat in his foot went away, but pain went everywhere. There was no abscess. He began to walk on the toe, not lowering the fetlock, and it was clear that the old bone chip had migrated into the joint cavity. Long before this event, nature might have handled the end of my old stallion's life better than I, more decisively, in its wise-kind-cruel-capricious fashion.

The inevitable is here. I will sell my Thoroughbred mare and ten-months old Anglo-Arab colt, and when they leave I will have Bayaref put to sleep. He has never been alone; while he's had only one mare and the current offspring for company for the past three years, he ran with a herd of mares and foals for nearly all his life (and whenever he could get away with it, he raided the other stallion's herd or adjoining pastures to add to his harem).

In March, I place a two-times ad in a monthly equine publication, figuring it will be well into the summer before I sell my 14-year old mare, and Bayaref will have the best part of spring to enjoy. Two weeks later, the first person to look at my mare wants her and the colt, and wants to bring her Arabian mare to breed to my stallion.

Most people cannot see past the trappings of old age in horses (or humans): the swayback, the protective shaggy winter coat, deep hollows above the eyes, and the quiet stance and lack of vigor that accompany conservation of energy. This buyer can.

"He's 28 YEARS OLD, you know," I tell her. "I have no idea whether he's still fertile this year." The buyer will take her chances, have her young mare checked by a vet, then bring her when she's due to come into season and take my mare and colt back across the state with her.

It is the sort of thing I might compose for an equine soap opera: my old friend's life (and a major part of mine) ending with a passionate fling with a teeny-bopper. Better to go out with a bang than a whimper . . .

She's a pleasant, funny, five year old maiden mare, intensely friendly and curious. She follows me about as I clean her stall, licks my jacket, puts her nose to mine and breathes my breath. I wonder about her stamina: her jaw is too narrow and she is slab-sided. Everything that could go wrong with the conformation of her hind end has. But she has nice long flat muscles, a good shoulder, and good symmetrical knees. It would be interesting to see what her foal would inherit.

The visiting mare's vet said she was going out of season, was on the last day when she arrived. In fact, it is the first day of her heat cycle. (Her vet also said this mare would not have settled before, because she was too young; I wish the vet had explained that to some accidentally pregnant yearling fillies I've known.)

Jewel stays in season for seven days, and after the first day she and my old stallion greet my arrival with anticipatory whinnies. They are waiting for me to hold her so the stallion can mount and breed her: his old hip and stifle joints can no longer cope with her taking a step or two. As he pumps away with little nickers and grunts and squeals of pleasure, I watch a throbbing jugular pulse the size of a ping pong ball, beating too fast, and I think that this would be a good way for an old horse to die. Best for all of us. But he finishes, slides off, and stands, utterly spent.

His pain is gone while the mare is in season--it's like giant doses of anabolic steroids. But within a day after he stops breeding the mare, the pain overwhelms him. He doesn't want to move. When he finally moves, he totters; the left front may hurt him the most, but every joint seems to be in agony. I go for more Butazolidin.

I am a newcomer in this area, so I have no easy camaraderie with a vet. The vet makes a big deal of an ordinary tube of Bute: "Big tube," she says, "lasts a long time at only one gram a dose." Hard to believe she used to work at the track, if she doesn't know the dose is, and has always been, one gram per 500 lbs of horse.

The Bute is gone in six days, and it has had little effect. Shall I ask for more? For something stronger? I would rather not see the veterinarian until I call her out to put my stallion down. First, because I may give way and seek invasive tests and prolonged treatment, when I know in my heart that would be wrong. Or I may break down and cry. And I lack rapport with her: When she said "don't worry, your pet won't feel any pain when I put him to sleep," the word "pet" offended me.

But then, she can't know that Bayaref has been my reliable friend and partner--and sometimes Atilla the Hun and sometimes Don Quixote, but no pet. She can't know my sadness at his predicament, and mine. I have had horses humanely destroyed in the past, but none that shared so much with me.

I must get Bayaref's pain under control, and I search for a household remedy before I return to the vet. I know aspirin won't work--it requires doses too large to manage. There's probably some study in the literature (I haven't kept up) about ibuprophen, probably dire side effects in horses: agranulocytosis, kidney failure, liver failure, whatever. Whatever, my old stallion has a couple of weeks of pain to live through, unless I call Jewel's owner to take her home now, before she's due back in season. Bayaref doesn't notice two dozen small ibuprophen tablets in his moistened feed.

There is an ancient bottle of Absorbine in the cabinet. Not Absorbine, Jr., but an old brown glass bottle with raised letters proclaiming "ABSORBINE 12 fl ounces," and the name and location of the manufacturer. It is so strong that I can smell it without opening the cabinet, and so old that I despair of ever getting its cap off. Opened, it brings tears to my eyes and clears my sinuses. I mix the evil-looking dark green liquid with DMSO and bathe all my stallion's hurting parts. He tries to flee the aromatic stench and the garlicky taste DMSO sends to his mouth (and mine), but nowadays I am quicker than he is. Then the warmth permeates (I can feel it too!) and he returns to his feed tub and eats voraciously.

Mornings, now, his pain is less under this regimen, so he goes out and tries harder and his pain becomes worse.

I always said Bayaref has a calendar in his head, although I acknowledge that it's probably just pheromones. When Jewel is due to come back into season, he asks her politely, then ignores her for two days. At the end of the third day, he notifies me that we're in business again.

Jewel's owner will pick her up in a week, on Monday. Every day, I have put two notes on my calendar: Call the vet. Call the knackers. Writing these things down erases them from my mind--until I return to the barn and confront misery.

I confront something else: I am not going to find Bayaref lying dead in his stall or in the pasture, at peace at last. His heart will not give out in a moment of passion, allowing him to exit in a final blaze of glory. He will never give up.

I dial. We agree on Tuesday morning. I am very calm; they are very kind.

Monday. I brush Bayaref and Jewel and turn them out to await Jewel's owner. For the first time, Bayaref takes Jewel all the way around the lake to the far side, a tortuous twenty-minute walk for him. They graze peacefully side by side, manes and tails lifted by the wind, backs kissed with silver by the morning sun.

I wait on the opposite bank. What if they turned the old caveat around to say "Today is the *last* day of the rest of your life"? Would we not be overcome with relief at having no choice in the matter? No relentless extortions to start all over again. No futile guilt that we have not done as well as we could've, would've, should've. No need to protest our innocence and our right to another chance to *prove* ourselves. We could say "I have fought the good fight, and that is that."

We have had a good life together. He was almost a perfect herd stallion, tolerating the playful antics of foals and weanlings kindly, patiently leading them in and out of vans and trailers, and rounding them up when they strayed too far. From all kinds of mares, Thoroughbreds, Arabs, Morgans, Quarterhorses, ponies, draft horses and coldbloods, Bayaref produced talented, tenacious, ambitious daughters, and handsome sons of average talent.

He loved mares and never abused one; he also coveted the

Thoroughbred stallion's mares, as well as all the mares on the farm. During the spring, summer and fall he watched for a chance to get into the seventeen-hand Thoroughbred stallion's pasture, fight him to the death, and steal his mares. A couple of times he managed to break out of his pasture and into the other stallion's, where a nasty fight ensued; and once he actually stole a little black mare from the Thoroughbred's herd, and drove her back over the broken fences into his herd. But when the first snow fell, Bayaref grew magnanimous towards his old rival. The little grey Arab would entice the big Thoroughbred over or through the fences and out into the lanes between their pastures, to wander about the farm and frolic in the snow like best friends.

He was a gentleman in public places, where few people realized he was a stallion. Only once, when he was five, did we have a problem stalling him away from home: Checking the stables, the owner of the show facility found Bayaref on top of a six-foot concrete block wall between him and an amorous mare, his front legs on one side and his back legs on the other. The owner kept her wits about her and said, sternly, "Bayaref, get down from there," and he did. He moved rather stiffly in his classes the next day.

He was too quick, too clever, too calculating for many horsemen, but with children and elderly ladies he was deliberately careful and gentle. Visitors to the barn were intrigued by the way he would stand in the back of his stall, watching them and listening to them, and nodding his head affirmatively whenever the conversation turned to him.

He had an honorable, if uneven, career. He won in unlikely events, and lost in others he should have aced, undone by his own zeal and ambition. He was his own worst enemy and my best friend, a very human horse.

The sound of Jewel's owner's truck and trailer interrupts my thoughts, and I realize that subconsciously I had hoped she would not come. I am comforted to learn that she has grown to love my mare, as I did, and that the mare is trotting nimbly over cavaletti as if she had done it all her life. The formerly docile Jewel is loaded into the trailer, vigorously protesting vocally and physically at leaving her lover. Her formerly reserved owner and I hug and weep briefly, then she drives away to a chorus of plaintive whinnies from Bayaref and Jewel.

Tuesday. Bayaref rests his head calmly against my breast while the veterinarian administers a massive intravenous shot of phenobarbital. He looks mildly surprised when he realizes that he is falling asleep, and we help him sink gently to the ground. There is no pain, no struggle or thrashing; he continues to breathe quietly, looking utterly at peace. After listening to his heart for several minutes, the vet says that his heart is so strong that she must give him more phenobarbital, and she does, then gently washes away the spot of blood from the injection. It is over. Bayaref looks oddly younger, even happy, and very peaceful, and I know that he is without pain and stress for the first time in a very long time.

A little later, I go back to reassure myself that he is at peace. To tell you the truth, I should not have been surprised to find him risen, wobbly but rested.

OLD FARMHOUSE FOR SALE

Here they come: the man who's already seen it and loves it, and his wife, who looks like she's sucking a lemon. I can almost hear her thoughts: "No way you are going to get me out *here* to live in an old farmhouse. I am going to have a 3-BR 2-BA brick ranch in a *good* neighborhood where everyone will know that I *belong*." Some days it's the wife who loves it and the husband who hates it; how can couples have such different tastes? Every time I get a matched pair that wants my little farm, they've got to sell their house first.

She's a little woman, not a hair out of place, lightly tanned, x-ray thin, and she keeps her arms folded across her chest. Two subdued children trail behind her, a boy and a girl about nine and ten years old, blonde like her. Her husband wears an uncertain smile and walking shorts that reveal a white pudginess hidden by a good suit on his first visit.

They come slowly up the steps, single file. The mother tries to step around the pecan flowerets littering the deck swept clean only an hour ago, and the kids cry "Yuck!" at the crunch beneath their feet. The giant pecan tree that shades my deck, kitchen and dining room is sharing its exuberant bloom.

"Sorry," I say, "They fall faster than I can sweep them up. I have to put up with this for a week in the spring, but no flowers, no pecans."

"In Moore County, they say there won't be any pecans this year."

"There will be a bumper crop here," I assure them, "about 400 pounds from this tree. See, these long flowers are the male flowers, and these little nubs," I pull a low hanging branch down to show them, "are fertilized female flowers already becoming pecans."

"Oh! Let me see the baby pecans!" The little girl is fascinated; her mother looks worried at this sexy talk. The father changes the subject:

"What happened to the trunk? Are those worm holes?"

"No, millions of woodpecker holes. All old pecan trees look like that." I lead them into the kitchen, quickly, before they notice the bird lime on the deck from the grackle nest hidden under the eaves.

She likes the huge kitchen. A bay window overlooks the deck and barn, the sink window overlooks the back lawn and pasture, and at the other end a fireplace is flanked by floor-to-ceiling bookshelves. She approves the separate laundry room behind the kitchen, but makes a face at the half of it cluttered with my tools.

Out the other kitchen door onto a small covered porch, I point out the perennials I planted in the dooryard. He says only "We would have to get someone out to spray those dandelions" and I picture the ten foot patch of dandelions wilting under a broadleaf weed killer, along with the Rose of Sharons, lilacs, Brown Turkey fig, gladiolus, hollyhocks and painted daisies, and the well that they surround poisoned. If they ask about the well and look down in it, this visit will be over.

But she looks only at the oak trees: "Hardwood trees are so messy."

"Yes," I agree, "but they provide shade in the summer and sunlight in the winter. And those big pines are messy all year round--actually, life in the country is messy!"

She likes the dining room's fireplace and double window and doesn't frown at the crowded corner where my computer perches equidistant between the television in the living room and the phone in the kitchen, but her face falls at the living room: "It's so small."

"All the rooms except the kitchen are the same size, 14'6" x 14'6"; that's typical of country homes built here in the twenties. And there's another living room or a fourth bedroom across the hall."

"I suppose we could take out this wall between the living room and dining room," she says, dubiously. Everyone wants to rip out my walls. I have learned not to distract them with phrases like "weight-bearing walls."

"Mom! Look!" Discovering a box of new kittens in the corner beside the television set, the subdued children come alive and dive for them. I dive after the kids.

"You can pet them and the mama cat, but don't pick them up, they're too young."

"Don't touch them, she might bite you!" the mother cries.

My little cat wakes up her kittens and curls around them, absolutely delighted to show them off. With her creamy Siamese coloring, bright blue eyes, one ear, and alley cat striped legs, she looks only dangerously ridiculous.

"What happened to her ear?"

"Ran under the mower when she was a kitten. Her name's Ms. Van Gogh." No one laughs.

"Too bad you don't have a garage to put them in," she says disapprovingly.

Before showing the rooms on the other side of the center hall, I open the door to the front porch, causing the black-capped chickadee who nests there to fly away. Wisteria and honeysuckle twine the railing and posts and hang suspended in mid-air, reaching for the windows and front door. My prospective buyers flinch from the waving tendrils. If I left the door open one night, I would not be surprised to find the vines creeping up the stairs by morning. I suppose I should cut them. Last year I cut them back to the ground, feeling guilty, and here they are, stronger than ever--but they smell good, and they're such vigorous, sociable vines.

"So close to the road," she murmurs.

"That's true, but the house was here long before the road was built. There is very little traffic."

"At least you have a chain link fence. What are those things growing on the fence?"

"Morning glories, luffa squash--which have giant yellow blossoms, and a couple of native vines--don't know their names but they have fragrant little white flowers that the bees love."

"Bees! Aren't you afraid of being stung?"

"No, honey bees are very peaceable." She would die if she knew about the hive in the chimney of the fourth bedroom.

"Who owns that property?" the husband nods at the calves standing chest-deep in the pretty lake across the road.

"A native of the area who lives two miles down the road. His daughter owns the house next to me."

"Is he black or white?"

"White," I say, trying not to show my anger. Last week, a young Jewish couple loved my little farm, stayed several hours, and raised my spirits by railing against the bigotry of this little corner of the South and planning how they would redecorate my house. I liked them immensely. The next day he phoned to say that other realtors told him that "only Indians and Blacks live out here; what are my neighbors?" Like most of the rural South, every fourth or fifth family here is Black or Indian, and most of them own their homes.

"Well," he says, pointing at my neighbor's ramshackle old barn with its tin roof flapping merrily in the breeze, "*that* will have to go."

Do these people think homeowner's association rules come with life in the country? Enough of the view from the front porch. I steer them quicky in and out of the fourth bedroom/parlor with the bee hive in its chimney, then down the hall to a bathroom where I apologize again:

"I use this bathroom for my darkroom." The trays and jugs are stashed under the sink today, but the acrid smell of the chemicals lingers.

As I whisk them through my bedroom, the chimney swifts that nest upon the damper in my fireplace twitter happily, but no one notices. The swifts sing off and on all night, a lovely song for a bird that looks like a flying cigar.

"I guess this is the master bedroom because I sleep here and it has its own bath." No one laughs. What if I told them about the lizard that slithers through a tiny space at the top of the storm window into my bathroom window every morning, and waits for flies to catch and eat? That my cat likes to drink from the toilet bowl and then lie on the window sill hoping to eat the lizard?

Upstairs, they view the first bedroom with approval, and the second, where my visiting grandchildren love to sleep because a chimney goes right through the middle of the room, with silent dismay.

"Old houses," I shrug, patting the chimney. "It would make a great bulletin board."

"There's no bathroom upstairs?"

"No, but then you don't have to worry about the children overflowing the tub." No one laughs. "Until the house was remodeled, 15 years ago, the only bath was a small room at the end of the laundry room, which was an open porch then."

At the end of the upstairs hall is a real attic, about 800 square feet with a big window, not a cramped space reached by pull-down stairs. They complain of the heat and eye the tin roof, rafters and planks suspiciously.

Thank God they probably won't want to tour the barn. I am sick of yuppies and city people who think it's weird to love an old house with personality and history instead of a stereotype in a "neighborhood," to prefer the mellifluent songs of hundreds of birds to the whine of weedeaters and the roar of mowers.

She re-examines the wall between the living room and dining room, studies the kitchen again. "How far is it to shopping?"I tell her it's ten miles to Moore County's overpriced supermarkets and chic shops, 30 miles to Fayetteville's big malls.

He says, "In Moore County, they say the schools over here are very bad."

"I've met a lot of the school officials here and I thought they were high caliber, although this is a small, poor county. Anyway," I shrug, "the schools in this state rank last in SAT scores, 48th in teacher pay, near the top in dropout rate and illiteracy. The kind of education your children get anywhere in this state will pretty much depend on your input. On the other hand, this property would cost you three times as much in Moore County, and what you would save on taxes alone would send one of your children to a very good private school in Moore County."

"Well, it is beautiful out here, but it's very different from what we are accustomed to."

"I know. And life in the country can be inconvenient, even hard sometimes. Country people make sacrifices--trade-offs-- for this kind of life." That was corny; I ought to quit preaching, keep smiling.

Back on the deck, the wife asks, "What kind of lily is that?"

"Elephant garlic," and when she frowns, I add: "It's delicious, expensive, and very hard to grow here." She looks approving, so I go on: "There's parsley next to it, and dogwood and sassafras in the yard and woods."

"What's that? It's moving!" The kids are jumping up and down, looking into the eaves. It looks like a fat grey electric wire dangling from the eaves. It is, however, the mottled grey and white belly of a snake. The snake's head is buried in the grackle's nest; a fatter loop of the snake contains three distinct lumps. The baby grackles are silent.

"Oh my God! Hubert, do something! Kill it!" Her tan has turned mottled grey and white, like the snake's belly.

I put a restraining hand on Hubert's arm: "Please, it's all right. The snake is not poisonous and it's just raiding a bird nest." The whole family looks mottled. "The grackles make two or three nests there during the summer; they'll start another family. It all works out: the birds eat the insects, and the snakes eat baby birds and eggs if they can get to them--but mostly the snakes eat mice."

The adults' faces reveal what they got out of this explanation: "Insects. Mice. Snakes eating baby birds."

"Thanks for coming," I say, "sorry about the snake--whoa, kids! Stop!" The kids have slipped off to the barn and are climbing over the fence; the yearling colts are approaching them with swift enthusiasm. I sprint after them.

"Stay on this side of the fence," I tell them. I don't want to hear any city kids howling, "Yuck, horse poop"--or worse, "horse shit;" don't want to explain again that it is *manure,* which is only digested grain and grass and very good for growing things; or have kids running up behind horses and getting their lights kicked out; or explain why they can't ride my ancient stallion, pregnant thoroughbred mare or yearlings. Each on his own side of the fence, children and horses exchange breaths and fondle each other until the parents catch up with us.

"We love it here! Mommy, Daddy, please buy it!"

"We'll see," Mommy says. She's still a sick snake-belly color. "We'd better be going; we have other places to look at."

"I can see where the north property line runs," Hubert says, "but where is the south line?"

For a moment, I contemplate taking them along the south line, teetering over the narrow board across the spring, squishing ankle deep through marsh, up the hill through the woods acquiring deer ticks as we go, then through the big patch of poison oak that's sprung up where we would have to climb over the fence. I would do it, but there is a mourning dove's nest at eye level near the spring, right next to the path; she would fly up, disturbed, and someone might touch the two white eggs in her nest.

"As you leave, you will see blue surveyor's tape marking the line, 250 feet past the end of the fence. If you decide that you are seriously interested in the property, come back and I will take you to walk the line."

The expensive car pulls away, slows politely near the blue surveyor's tape, then speeds off to a world that doesn't know about the owl that hoots in the marsh by day or the anxious calls of the whippoorwills at night, or the joyous songs of the mockingbirds all day long. A world that doesn't care that the bluebirds have returned and the barn swallows are building a new mud nest in the yearling colt's stall. Or about drought and rain and shallow wells; old trees that protect a home; stinging horse flies and rolling green pastures. Learning to identify poisonous plants. The good things that spring out of the ground. Root cellars and spring houses. Mending fences on the hottest and coldest days of the year. The satisfaction of learning, one at a time, 101 emergency repairs to avert disaster; the sheer terror of the 102nd disaster. A world that doesn't know two of my best neighbors, a Lumbee Indian, and a Black whose family has owned land here for a hundred years. A world that will never know about the mourning dove.

ALONE IN THE DARK

A funny thing happened on my way to the computer. The electricity went off. I was helpless in the dark with thoughts ricocheting madly inside my head about that little piece of a story that I couldn't finish last week and I couldn't retrieve the story from the computer disks. Nor could I make a cup of coffee, cook supper, or brush my teeth--in the country no electricity means that no water will be pumped from the well. Still, one must do *something* until the lights come on.

What I did was light a candle and get pen and paper, and rediscover that words composed by pen and candlelight are intrinsically personal, not just crisp manipulation of readers' minds with facile keyboard and computer chip. I thought about what we did when the electricity failed before all the kids left home: we celebrated the adventure of the darkness and the excuse for not working. We talked, and we listened to each other and to the mysterious and the friendly sounds of the night. By candles and kerosene lamps we played bridge, rummy or scrabble, or whatever we had enough players for, for however long it took before the lights came on or somebody fell asleep or went blind.

Being alone in the dark now is neither an adventure nor even a fright, just an inconvenience and a bore. Maybe my inner resources left when the kids did.

I always figured that if a parent did a halfway decent job of raising kids, they'd leave home someday. My five children each left home several times, practicing until they got it right, I suppose. The trouble with those multiple departures was that I liked teenagers and enjoyed the company of my own young adults more and more as they grew older. Nevertheless, I occasionally thought about "freedom," picturing carefree days in a clean, organized home. I had a lot to learn.

The hard lesson turned out to be that freedom flourishes only where there are loving ties. The other lessons have been more amusing. Like the idea that the litter and dirt that children distribute generously throughout a household were going to be gone when the kids were. Wrong. It turned out that I was the litterer, too busy to notice, by nature disinclined to assign blame, and spoiled by many hands making light work. Now that I lack an appreciative audience, my cleaning routine depends upon whether dust threatens my computer and my film processing.

I'll never get food-for-one right.

Leftovers just like those we used to fight over undergo strange changes nowadays--the cure for the common cold may be growing in my refrigerator. The leftovers that don't reach back when I reach for them never seem go with anything else, which leads to combinations like kielbasa, noodles, red peppers, broccoli and sour cream (the colors are nice).

Take cantaloupe: the first quarter is a treat, the next three a duty--especially if it wasn't a great melon. And milk: I can almost pace my milk consumption to match the expiration date on the jug, if I can resist buying four pints of Half & Half on sale for a dollar. I thought it would be fun to eat whatever you want when you want it. Candy was fun when chocolate was for special occasions and I had to protect the children's teeth and my waistline. When I walked in the house after sneaking a chocolate bar, the kids' noses would twitch like rabbits' before they wailed, "Mother! You've been eating chocolate!" Chocolate doesn't taste the same now.

God knows, all those great pots of hearty, artery-clogging food were a lot of planning and budgeting, chopping and stirring and washing up, but we shared more than food at the long table. Nothing tastes as good without that magic ingredient, sharing.

If there were anyone to share the dark, to cling to while fierce winds shake this old house and the lightning hunts for a plugged-in computer or answering machine, chances are *I'd* be comforting *him*. Chances are, nothing would come of the tension shared intimately by two people trapped in a storm: my male peers freely complain that they can't get it up or keep it up; I suspect they'd rather talk about it than try it. It's no wonder they can't perform, most of them are in such terrible shape that undressing would unveil a natural disaster. Then there is the awkward prerequisite broaching of one's sexual history and health. How carefree sex was before AIDS; how final the sad metamorphosis of sex.

Something's gone wrong with my plans for discretionary income. I thought I'd have more money and more fun spending it when there was only me to look after. Wrong again. Now that I have acquired a lifetime of experience and have no distractions to keep me from giving an employer my best, I am worth a great deal less on the job market and everything costs a great deal more.

My first tentative venture into discretionary spending took place when I still had family responsibilities: I took flying lessons. At the end of a soaring summer, I had to borrow $140 from my oldest daughter to have an impacted, infected wisdom tooth excavated. "Mother," she cried, "how *could* you take flying lessons when you knew you had to take care of that wisdom tooth!"

Some of my "discretionary" income went for a German Shepherd puppy, which demonstrates how little I learned in several years of living alone. However, I learned a lot from the puppy, like why my children always owned the dogs and cats and how good they were at taking care of them. It easy to tell your child that the wet/muddy/flea-infested dog cannot

186

come inside; it is impossible to look at those loving eyes and thumping tail and tell the dog yourself. Bathing and de-fleaing the dog is a minor task when the kids do it. It is much better for a dog, like a person, to have several people to love instead of just one.

Living alone puts mothers out of the martyr business. There is no appreciation for doing the unpleasant and boring jobs, and not much chance to do those special tasks that uplift doer and recipient. And then there is pain and suffering: living with large animals and working on pastures, fences and barns, one gets bashed from time to time. When you get bashed before the kids leave home, you get a little comfort and pampering. When you tell the kids about it after they leave, it is whining. Just mentioning the routine aches and pains of these golden years is hypochondria.

When you live alone, "things" can take on lives of their own. My 11-year-old computer system had only failed me once, when lightning took out its mother board, but it had gotten more updates than an organ bank. When the technician stuck a "Do Not Resuscitate" sticker on it, I realized that my faithful old servant had assumed the status of a family member. Even after getting a new computer and printer, I kept the old system in a closet for a year. Rather like keeping grandfather's ashes on the mantel.

I recall fondly the idiosyncrasies and indestructibility of ancient tractors, horse vans, sewing machines, toasters, and typewriters. I could write about the souls of old machines, but I'm afraid of the religious right.

A well-insured motorist ran a red light and totaled my 12-year-old, 195,000 miles-on-its-odometer Toyota pickup (but not me). Her insurance company offered me $1,000 more than the Blue Book value of my pickup, but I very much wanted my old Toyota restored to its former glory, which included paint faded from its original burgandy to lusterless brown;

assorted dents; an often caulked and still leaky camper top; upholstery worn through on the driver's side; stick-shift transmission; a radio with a range of two stations; uncomfortable seating for one and misery for two; and failed air conditioning.

I saw all that, and saw more clearly an old friend that had all its original parts and always got me from here to there. It is hard to relinquish the "things" that have enabled and extended us.

Then I saw a "For Sale" sign in my neighborhood for a 4-door Subaru one year older but 75,000 miles younger in wear. It had an electric sun roof and windows, comfortable adjustable seats, good paint, and more bells, knobs and whistles than I had ever seen. It was almost $1,000 less than the insurance company would give me to consign my old pickup to that great junkyard in the sky. A no-brainer.

It took me a couple of months to understand why I missed my disreputable-looking pickup. When I drove the pickup, strangers waved to me. Other cars got out of my way - who wants to incur liability from an old wreck? I knew and respected its limitations, and it never failed me. There was a memory attached to each dent. My old pickup was more than a means of transportation: it was an attitude, a statement.

Nobody waves to in my new car, but the bells and knobs and whistles all work and the mileage is okay. If only I didn't feel so ordinary and fuddy-duddy driving it.

On the other hand, I used the profit on my old pickup to publish this book instead of soliciting publishers, because rejection is another "thing" that grows larger than life when you are alone in the dark.

The worst part of living alone is what I call the sounding board syndrome: the loss of all human reactions to the trivial as well as the catastrophic. The loss of acceptance, caring, shock, outrage, intelligent curiosity and, most of all, humor.

Is "sounding board syndrome" the reason that people who live alone are often humorless, or are they living alone because they never had a sense of humor?

The lights have come back on. Please tell me that you are laughing.